I0668953

In this vivid, moving collection, Mark Lewandowski brings us the tough poetry of the Alaskan fishing industry, an end-of-the-world ecosystem of Slime-Line Queens and drunks, Born-Agains and sinners. Like the fish workers he describes, Lewandowski knows how to eviscerate. He peels back his characters' thick skins and removes their still-beating hearts. *Halibut Rodeo* is an arresting collection of stories about lonely people trying to find each other and hold on.
– Lili Wright, author of *Learning to Float*

Welcome, traveler from the Lower Forty-Eight, to the land of strange names—Kachemak Bay, Homer Spit, Kodiak, Kenai Mountains—and stranger jobs where people work the slime line and build glaciers out of frozen fish. Let Mark Lewandowski show you, in these fine stories, the ice, the cold, the smell of the Alaska salt as he ultimately guides you deeper into the odd people of this place, and you recognize them as everyone you have ever known, and finally catch glimpses of the traveler that you are.
–Marlin Barton, author of *A Broken Thing*

Lewandowski's delightful collection, *Halibut Rodeo*, may be set in the cold climes of Alaska's canneries, but each story here has enough humor and heart to warm any reader. Where Steinbeck's *Cannery Row* meets 'The Deadliest Catch,' this debut proves that humanity endures even at the farthest reaches of civilization.
–Peter Charles Melman, author of *Landsman*

HALIBUT RODEO

Mark Lewandowski

ALL THINGS

THAT MATTER

PRESS

HALIBUT RODEO

Copyright © 2010 by Mark Lewandowski

All rights reserved. No part of this book may be reproduced or transmitted in any form or by any means without written permission of the author and publisher.

This is a work of fiction. Any resemblance to actual persons, living or dead, is purely coincidental.

ISBN 13: 9780984421930

Library of Congress Control Number: 2010903593

Cover design by All Things That Matter Press

Published in 2009 by All Things That Matter Press

For Ma and Dad

Acknowledgments

Personal Acknowledgement:

I'd like to thank the teachers and readers who taught me how to do this: Lee K. Abbot, James Lee Burke, Mahlon Coop, Carolyn Doty, James Gunn, Tom Lorenz, Hans Montelius, Kathy Roberts, Nancy Roberts, Bob Shacoshis, and Mark Smith.

Professional Acknowledgments:

Some of the stories in this book first appeared in the following magazines: "The Slime-Line Queen," Writers' Forum; "Breaking the Halibut," The Potomac Review; "The Prince of Kodiak," The Red Cedar Review; "A Man Loves His Cat," Pinyon; "To War" (as "To War! To War!"), The North American Review; "The First Snow of Spring," Eureka Literary Magazine; "Substitutions," RE:AL.

Table of Contents

The Slime-Line Queen 1

Breaking the Halibut... 19

The Prince of Kodiak 31

King Salmon 47

A Man Loves His Cat.. 61

To War 71

The First Snow of Spring 81

In The Hands of Heaven... 87

Substitutions.. 101

The Slime-Line Queen

I caught a break from case-up and was sent over to the slime-line where I stood on a platform and flipped giant halibut onto their dull green topsides, making sure the gaping, bloody triangular gouge that used to be the face was in front before I shot the bottom fish down a ramp and onto the conveyor belt that fed the slimers below. The slimers dragged the fish from the belt and dug and scraped out the bloodline with two-bladed knives that spit water from their handles onto the serrated edges. From my heightened position I surveyed the slimers: those men too small and fragile to handle the frozen fish weighing a hundred pounds and more in case-up; the older women who let the bigger fish pass them by to hog the smaller and easier ones; the Russian women in their long, printed skirts and blouses who never got dirty and never worked on Sundays, even though it usually paid overtime. All the slimers were somber, their ivory faces like day-old whipped cream, all but the Russians looking like bruised bananas in their piss yellow rain gear. All, that is, except one. This one had a touch of red in her cheeks, and her occasional throaty giggle ripped through the roaring of the forklifts and hacksaws, driving a wedge into the muffled chaos inside my headphones. She was taller than all the other women slimers, and she looked much younger. Her sleeves were streaked with coagulated blood, and her hair was tucked under-neath a checkered red bandanna. She attacked each halibut with zeal, as if she were the one who was going to eat it, and when she came across a male with its balls still firmly implanted, she stuffed her arm into the hole and ripped out the white scrotum with a smile. She then placed it, like a trophy, on top of the housing covering the brushes designed to clean excess slime from the fish. Sometimes a fish got caught in there and with one hand she pulled it out and slid it through, and with the other hand she picked up a sac and winged it at a slimer across from her. She was exciting to watch; she was flam-boyant, she was the Slime-Line Queen of Homer, Alaska.

I was in love.

After I flipped the last fish I was told to punch out. The second halibut run was a bust. Salmon were starting to trickle in, but since I was new, I wouldn't get to work for a few days, much to my disappointment. My whole body ached from lack of sleep and from slinging around fish heavier than most humans. But, for some perverse reason I almost enjoyed the mindless activity of working the line that disassembled fish. I had been in college for four years, and never during that time did I feel like I was actually doing anything. Maybe that's why I was immediately attracted to the Slime-Line Queen; she made cleaning fish an art. I hoped to talk to her after work, but she was sent over to the salmon line. There were only a few totes of fish lined up; she wouldn't be long. I decided to take my chances and wait and see if she, like many others from Seward Fisheries, would pop up at the Salty Dawg Saloon afterward.

***

The Salty Dawg was a bar with character. The old wooden building was a converted lighthouse, the lamp still shining on foggy days, and walking across the sawdust-covered floors I had to duck to avoid the low beams holding up the dilapidated roof. After the first halibut run, the Dawg was a great place to get free drinks from fishermen right off the ocean, still reeking with their catch, their pockets bulging with cash, or to get a job repairing nets or scrubbing an oily dock. But the second run was less successful, and the same fishermen who drank to excess and who bought the entire bar rounds the month earlier now sat huddled in dark corners, nursing domestic drafts and mumbling to the carved up walls, as if the memories etched there could reflect the upcoming salmon run.

I bought a Chinook Ale and walked to the back of the bar. Larry, who could usually be found holding a map of the Himalayas against the wall as he traced raggedy red lines around the mountains, now sat expressionless, a line of empty shot glasses in front of him. Alfred, a Native from Kodiak who once guided grizzly hunters, was next to him, as quiet as ever.

"Hey," I said, sitting down at a table next to them. "Why worry about today when tomorrow's only going to be worse?"

My two companions sat there like mummies.

So I waited, searching the same invisible spaces as they. I drank three ales while Larry and Alfred threw back shots of whiskey. I turned to look into Larry's eyes. That could be me in there, I mused. Forty and comatose. He twitched. I jerked my gaze back to the front of the bar and watched her saunter in.

The red bandanna she wore on the slime-line to cover her hair was now wrapped around her long neck, her dirty blond curls tucked into the folds. She sported an old, worn out red and white flannel shirt that streamed past her hips, making them appear very wide. Her face was creamy, and even though her blue eyes were pale, they sparkled like a glacier under a full moon.

She came in with two men shorter than her; they stood to one side of her at the bar. I placed my half-empty bottle on the ground and went up to the bar for another.

"Hi!" she said; it came out in two, exaggerated syllables, the second tailing off, much longer than the first, and reaching a much higher note. If you could draw her "hi" on paper, it would look like a curli-cue.

"Hi," I said, and paused. "You work at the plant, don't you?"

"Wait! I know you," she said, then bit her pinky. "You're the one who kept sending me all those halibuts. I hate doing those. You must not be very nice." Her tongue jutted out of her mouth, and she laugh-ed as the bartender poured her a double tequila.

I couldn't picture her face without a smile.

"What are you doing during salmon?" I asked. "Do you know yet?" For such a large woman she had small teeth.

"Sliming!" It came out like her "hi." Curlicue.

The bartender returned and dropped a quarter of lime in front of her. I ordered an ale.

"I suppose that's what I'll be doing too..." But she didn't hear me, or at least she didn't respond. One of her friends said something, funny I suppose, because she turned to him laughing and placed a hand on his chest. With the smile still on her face, the corners of her eyes crinkling like cellophane, she bit into the lime, set the edge of the glass between her puckered lips, gently tipped it back, then again bit into the lime.

"Can I get you another?" I asked.

"That's so sweet." She looked me in the eyes. "But I only have one a night." She turned back to the empty glass and ran her finger along the rim. Her hands looked much older than her face: prominent veins, patchy brown skin, dull and ragged fingernails.

"Oh," I said.

She turned back to me, picked up the lime and ran it across her lips. She giggled, like she did at work, a throaty giggle, like the roar of a baby lion.

"You know," she said. "The girls were talking about you after work."

"About what?"

"Everyone thinks you're cute."

"No, they don't." I placed two dollars on the bar and grabbed the frosted bottle.

"Yes! Don't you know that you are?"

I blushed, shrugged. When I tried to catch her eyes she was once again laughing and petting that guy's chest.

"They're just saying that," I said.

She turned back to look at me.

"They're just saying that because I'm the new kid on the block."

She considered this for a moment, and then simply said: "Maybe."

"Listen," I said. "Do you want to go out and get something to eat?" Too fast, I thought. I don't even know her name.

"You're so sweet." She touched my arm with her wet fingers. "But we're all going over to Addie's Big Patties."

She rubbed her friend's ass with her thigh.

"Why don't you come with us?"

"Right now?"

"In a bit."

"Okay," I said. "I'll be back in a sec."

Before I entered the john I looked back, but she was once again absorbed in laughter with her friends.

Addie's Patties, I thought. I could take her to Land's End for steak and halibut, a nice bottle of wine.

When I returned from the john my eyes fell on the empty spot at the bar, the bottle of ale I had just ordered sitting there alone, her glass and lime taken away, she and her companions gone.

Maybe I should have stayed and got drunk. Or maybe I should have shoved aside my humiliation and just showed up at Addie's. Instead, I resolved to call it a night and forget all about the Slime-Line Queen. I left the Salty Dawg, and then paused to gaze at the Kenai Mountains across Kachemak Bay. I had been in Alaska for six weeks, but was still mesmerized by the snow-covered mountains that grew out of the water like hurricane waves. The peaks were only a couple thousand feet above sea level, and seemed like they'd be easy things to ascend, but their points were sharp, their sides blanketed with snow, and through their valleys ran thick and ancient glaciers. Cross the bay, I thought, and I'd be at the top of the world. I shook my head and remembered the view of downtown Buffalo from my basement apartment there: the trapped, nauseating fumes left behind from factories long deserted, the rocking explosions from mufflerless cars, hookers and crack dealers setting up shop across the street, very near a high school. My life there seemed very far away.

I walked down the road connecting Homer Spit to the rest of town, past elevated boardwalks supporting halibut charters and sourdough bakeries. Fifteen minutes after I left the Salty Dawg I was on the fringes of Tent City, or Spit Rat City, my home for the summer. The City was located on a piece of beach Sew-Fish leased out for its employees. When David, my buddy from Buffalo, and I arrived in May, only a dozen tents were bunched up around the makeshift community living room: a big pit used to cook Dolly Vardens, surrounded by driftwood couches. But as July approached, with its promise of long hours during salmon season, the beach filled up. Now, fifty or sixty tents were scattered around the original settlement.

Nicole, a graduate student from Reed College, squatted in the sand and sang songs to the dark waves, as she had all summer long. I nodded to her and treaded the familiar path past the tent that was always opened toward the sea, where Ted, as usual, banged one of the

5

teenaged girls who hung around the plant. They were splayed out on a moldy bean bag chair. Filling flew out in puffs through its tears. Ted gave me a thumbs up. I continued, past a guy who launched pieces of halibut to bald eagles with a sling shot; past the tent that sported a spiker-like houka in plain view of the road; past the tent of the dealer, who always kept his gear locked away and ready to move; past the homemade sauna that was nothing but a sheet of moldy plastic hitched up on sticks above a pot, a concoction the mayor of Homer called an eyesore; and finally to the Living Room where my fellow Spit Rats boiled Dungeness crab and drank from a keg of Chinook Ale.

David was the buddy who convinced me to join up for this Alaska venture. He and I shared a tent buried halfway into the rocky sand. The side facing the sea was barricaded with driftwood. Sleep sounded awfully good, but I knew by the moans and rustlings emanating from the tent that David was entertaining Barbara, a woman he had met on the herring line.

"For Chrissake," I said. "Can't you ever go to her place?"

"Take my pot," David called out.

"There's a good substitute for sleep," I said. But I picked up the belt pouch he had left by the tent flaps, and jogged out to the shoreline to smoke a joint and dream about the Slime-Line Queen.

***

When the salmon season hit full stride, I was placed on the slime-line. We worked twenty straight days, up to sixteen hours a day. We were given fifteen-minute breaks every two and a half hours, and as the days rolled by, the break room, once full of laughter and energy, became quiet and still. After the first day of sliming, tendonitis crept into my right wrist and hand. By the third day the pain had spread into my left hand, the feeling in all my fingertips reduced to occasional pinpricks.

Like everyone else, I combated the pain with a steady stream of Advil. However, there was no effective way to fight the job's monotony. The salmon never stopped coming. Slowly, they rolled down the belt, guts hanging out of their pre-sliced bellies. We grabbed them by the neck with one hand, tore out their insides with the other, and then scrapped out the bloodlines with a curved knife. Because the fish came in ice cold, after a few fish our hands became the same, even with thickly lined gloves. Cold or not, with pain or not, a good slimer was expected to clean four or five fish a minute. After just a few fish all of us were completely covered in blood, and bits of intestine dripped from our white faces. When we worked too slowly, the fish piled up at the end of the belt before sliding over the barrier and falling to the floor with a splat. Some of the slimers amused themselves by flinging salmon hearts at each other, using the bloody knives as crude catapults. One girl, with brown, puppy dog eyes, looked around wildly before squashing the hearts with the hilt of her knife. I spent the many hours wondering what it would be like to work at a place like this for a living, wondering if college was preparing me for anything else.

It took me a week to find out that the Slime-Line Queen was working in the egg room, packing the precious orange balls for the Japanese, who believed them to be aphrodisiacs. I was told only the meticulous and most experienced worked in the egg room. You had to have flair, and only company people were considered, at least that's what they told me when I tried to transfer over there.

On the nineteenth day, she finally, suddenly, arrived on the line. She squeezed in across from me, talked loud and fast to the person on her right, and with strong swipes of her knife the bloodlines shot out of the salmon and plastered the slimer on her left. She gutted as fast as she talked, letting neither activity break the rhythm of the other.

She doesn't remember me, I thought. But the moment the supervisor yelled, "Break time!" a salmon heart bounced off my forehead and dropped in front of me. I blinked, looked across the belt, and saw her glaring at me with a smile.

***

"I'm Paul," I said, holding out my hand. We were sitting at one of the tables in the break room.

7

"You're so cute!" she said, looking down at my hand. "Besides, I know that." She opened the same red and white flannel shirt and took out a blue packet of Drum tobacco from a brown corduroy pocket sewn inside. She quickly rolled a cigarette and tossed me the bag.

I couldn't manage the frail rolling paper with my numb hands.

"I'm afraid I don't know yours," I said, dumping tobacco in my lap. She laughed and took the lit cigarette out of her mouth and gently placed it between my lips.

"Michele." She rolled a cigarette for herself.

"Michele. That's a pretty name." I pulled on the cigarette and noisily coughed out the smoke. I hadn't had tobacco since high school.

She giggled and brushed my shoulder with her hand.

When she smoked, her neck arched back, and she took long, slow, deep drags, her lips placing virtually no pressure on the unfiltered cigarette, so when she finally removed it from her mouth the tip was still perfectly rounded. She paused before exhaling, again arching her neck so the thin stream of smoke exploded in a thick cloud on the ceiling.

She caught me staring, and when she talked again her voice had lost its curlicue.

"What's your story?" she asked softly.

"My story?"

"Everyone has a story, everyone here. Since you're living in Tent City, I assume you're from Outside."

I shrugged.

"I'm just a college student. Making money. That's all."

She said nothing for a moment, seemed almost disappointed.

"Married?" she asked. Her voice had changed again, grown deeper, as if she were speaking from a distance. I'm not sure if it mattered to her.

"No," I answered, and then said hesitantly: "But, ah, how did you know my name and where I'm staying?"

She shrugged and said, "Small town." With her cigarette, she burned a hole into a crumpled Snickers wrapper.

"Well, then," I said. "What's your story?"

"I don't have one," she said. For a moment, for the briefest pause, the age from her hands spread upward into the skin beneath her eyes.

I didn't know what to say. I hoped that she had reached the same conclusion as me, that our lives were probably similar.

Michele looked over my shoulder, as if searching for something. Before anything else could be said, though I don't think any "thing" would have been said, the supervisor came in.

"All right, butcher crew!" he said. "It looks like we have one shift left for the day..."

Before he finished, Michele had kicked out her chair and placed the smile back onto her face. She winked at me, and we stomped down the stairs together to slip into our bloody rain gear.

***

Again, the next day, the twentieth workday in a row, Michele simply popped into existence across from me, toward the end of the shift. Yet, she still attacked the fish with vigor.

"What's the deal," I asked during break. "Why don't you start on the line?"

"Politics."

"Politics?"

"It's the Japanese. They supervise the egg room, you know. They think I have too much fun. Imagine that." Michele took the tobacco from the same pocket within the same shirt.

"I thought you just needed a change, any change. I can't imagine the egg room being much better."

"But it is. It's easy." She scraped a bit of tobacco from the bottom of the pack and rolled a pin joint, then sucked it down in two drags.

"Well, I could use a break," I said.

She looked down at my curled fingers. I tried to straighten them by pressing them flat on the table.

"Tomorrow is a day off," she said.

"Are you sure?" I asked. "I mean, I've heard rumors."

"I think we should plan on it," she said.

"We?"

***

I must have awoken when the whistling from the teakettle died out, all the water boiled away. I propped myself up on my elbows and tossed the can of International Foods coffee back into the bag with the other things I had purchased for the evening, my first off in three weeks: a half pound of macadamia nuts, a bottle of white zinfandel, a triangle of brie.

I hadn't talked to Michele since the night before, during break. I just missed her after work as she thumbed down an El Camino a hundred yards in front of me, leaving me wondering what she had meant by "planning" for a day off.

I had wandered around that day, carrying my groceries, hoping to run into her by chance. I even bought three condoms at seventy-five cents apiece, thinking a whole box would be presumptuous.

"Where the hell did everybody go?" I fired into the air. The Living Room was empty, and the purple, starless night was quickly approaching. It appeared that even David, who worked night case-up and who was looking more like a walking vegetable every day, had pulled himself out of bed and joined the party that had started in the City and continued God knows where.

I opened a beer and flipped the cap into a small pile of bottles I had emptied earlier.

I sat back against a drift log and took the condoms out of my pocket, then tossed them into my opened tent. Fatigue began again to overtake me. I drank my beer and lazily popped macadamia nuts into the fire, waiting for small explosions that never occurred.

As I began to doze once again, a throaty giggle, distant but loud, blew the clouds out of my head.

"You're so cute!" Michele said from the road. A moment later, she plopped down in front of me.

"Hi!" she said, looking around. "Nice place."

"Well, yeah. Thanks. I don't know where anybody is."

"They're at Alice's Champagne Palace. I thought for sure you'd be there."

"You looked?"

"Of course." She placed her hand on my thigh. "I told you we should plan on the day off. But it's getting late now. No day off tomorrow."

"No." I pushed the bag of stuff behind me.

"I didn't see you in town, so I hitched here," she said.

"Oh."

"Something the matter?"

"Me? No, no I'm just tired. That's all."

"So am I." She folded her arms around her bent knees and rocked. "So why don't you spend the night with me?"

***

We hitched a ride off the spit in a small pickup, Michele laughing with the driver up front, the ocean wind tearing into my clothes in back. He dumped us at the edge of Beluga Lake, between a floatplane service and McDonald's. As we walked, I found out that Michele had been living in Alaska for two years, and had little inclination to return to her family's farm in South Dakota. She didn't tell me why.

We crossed the Homer bypass and entered the thick woods behind the post office. Our hands occasionally brushed against each other's, and the fourth or fifth time I grabbed hers.

"Rub it," she said.

"What?"

"Massage my hand," she said. "It hurts."

I slowed our pace and massaged her hand with both of mine.

"You're so up all the time," I said. "I didn't think you were affected."

She smile quickly, without showing her teeth, then gazed into the shadows that had wrapped themselves around the pine trees.

"I don't plan on doing this forever," she said, but without much conviction.

She pulled her hand back and walked faster. As we rounded a curve in the path, dark, boxy cabins emerged from the trees. Michele lived in the second one and she pushed open the unlocked door.

The cabin was only one room, with no bathroom. The little wall space not taken up by cupboards was covered with posters of half-naked male television stars. There were no chairs, only a king-sized mattress below a large, curtainless window, and a braided hammock that hung from the ceiling, both ends tied around the same hook.

Michele mixed together wine and orange juice and served it to me in a clay beer stein.

I pulled her into my arms and kissed her, but she wouldn't open her mouth to meet my tongue.

"What was that for?" she asked, easing away.

"I just felt like doing it, I guess."

"It was nice." She sat on the bed and turned on the little black and white television.

"Maybe I should go now," I said.

"Go?" She stood up. "You just got here, and you said you'd spend the night."

"I guess I thought you changed your mind."

She took my elbow in her hand.

"I just want you to comfort me," she pleaded.

"Well, I thought...Okay, whatever."

I dropped down on the bed.

She peeled off her jeans and flannel shirt. Underneath were a black body suit and white spandex leggings.

I don't get this, I thought.

"Get out of those clothes," she demanded. "Or do you usually sleep in your jeans?"

I unbuckled my belt and reached for the condoms in my shirt pocket, but of course they weren't there.

She stuck her finger through one of my belt loops.

"If you don't take these off, I will," she said.

As I rolled the jeans off my legs, I felt the same combination of horror and delight I had every time I was about to make love: a mixture of extreme nervousness and anticipation.

She dropped three blankets over me, then tucked me in and slid in next to me.

She cuddled up against me, back toward me.

12

"Hold me," she said. "Hold me tight."

I wrapped my arms around her and pressed my erection between her legs.

"God!" She raised her head.

"I'm sorry," I said.

"Don't be. I'm comfortable if you are."

"I don't have anything with me," I said.

She didn't respond, just dropped her head back into her pillow.

I waited. But Michele didn't move, didn't touch me, but didn't struggle either.

Hold me tight, she had said. So I did, and shortly started to doze, with her holding onto my arms, but wanting nothing more.

A few minutes, or maybe a few hours later, I felt Michele draw away from me.

"What. Where are you going?" I looked up and saw the moonbeams pouring through the window, washing her face with a white glow, the rest of her body cloaked in shadow.

She let out a deep breath and said: "You might want to see this."

I sat up and looked out the window. We both moved closer, until our noses touched the cool glass, our arms around one another.

"My God," I said.

Not more than five feet from our faces stood a moose, her snout buried in a potted plant sitting on the ground. Clinging to her side, like stuffed toys, were two calves, standing on impossibly thin legs, their snouts dropping occasionally to nip a bit of grass. I raised my hand and rested my numb fingertips on the window. I thought I could smell the husky perfume of the moose.

"She's beautiful," I said. The words did little to describe the sense of peace that had settled over me.

Michele and I watched until the potted plant was eaten, and the three visitors had lumbered away into the woods, its shadows embracing them in darkness.

We slid back into bed and pulled the covers over us.

"Are you comfortable, Paul?"

"Yes, yes. Very much so. Are you?"

"Mmmm."

We embraced, front to back again, and I fell into a deep, secure sleep.

***

Bonus was called on August third. Salmon season was officially over and workers could take voluntary lay-offs while retaining full bonus checks. I had a ticket to leave Anchorage on the tenth, leaving me a week with Michele. Unless I went the same route as David; he had sold his ticket and was ready to move in with Barbara.

The week and a half since Michele and I spent our night together passed much like the first part of the season; we were left too exhausted to do anything but talk in snippets during breaks, or have a quick drink together at the Dawg after work. But when I did see her, the warmth I had experienced that first night came rushing back to me. And in many ways, I caught onto her enthusiasm, and work flew by. I remained fatigued and in pain, but began to look forward to work, knowing I would get to see Michele there.

The day after bonus was called, the Spit Rats began to break down the City. David's gear was packed and ready for a rented mobile home. I took the airline ticket from my money belt. The ticket had torn at a crease, and the red backing bled through and left splotches across the numbers. Nevertheless, the departure time and destination were still clear. I dropped the ticket into my shirt pocket.

That day, Sew-Fish held a company picnic in a park overlooking the entirety of Homer and a good part of Kachemak Bay. The sky was clear and the Kenai Mountains were glowing, as if filled to their peaks with stars. Michele and I talked a bit before the dinner of Silver salmon and Dungeness crab, but she had many friends there, not all female, and I never thought I captured her attention until we got a softball game going and I made a diving, bare-handed catch in centerfield. She jumped off the bleachers, cheering and yelling my name. But afterward, while she played on the opposing team in volley ball, I watched her through the net, joking with and touching the guys, guys who, like her, lived in Homer all year round, or others who had been coming up to work every summer for years. I drank more and more beer, and after the volley ball game, I convinced Alfred the Native to get on the teeter-totter with me. I stood balanced on one side, beer in hand, while he started from the middle and slowly edged to the other side. He was much bigger than me, and after a few attempts of trying to remain steady, both of us level and in the air at once, he did something to bring all of his weight down. I flipped off my end and went sprawling to the hard ground. Michele started laughing from a distance, and as I stood up, brushing off the dirt and massaging my torn and bloodied elbows, she greeted me with a fresh beer.

"That was cute!" she said.

"Thanks." I pulled the shirt, wet with beer, from my skin, then took out the plane ticket and rubbed it dry on my jeans.

"My ticket to go back," I said. "My friend David sold his. Most people bought one-way tickets up, or hitched the Alaska Highway, or took the ferry from Seattle. They're in great demand." I held the ticket up to the darkening sky.

Michele looked back to the shelter where everyone was starting to eat.

"David wants to get married," I said. "It's not like him, but what the hell."

Michele brought her attention back to me.

"Barbara's sweet," she said.

"Yeah," I said. I waited for her to make the move, to give me some indication that she wanted me to stay. I needed help. I took her beer, and placed both of ours on the ground. I held onto her hands, caressing them gently. She glanced back to the shelter.

"They still hurt?" I asked.

"They always hurt," she replied, with a sharpness I hadn't heard before.

"Mine too," I said.

"By the time you write your first paper this year in college," she said, "you'll forget all about it."

"Yeah," I started.

"Come on," she said, her voice changed, now high and every word filled with a curlicue. "Everybody's eating!" The glow came back to her face, and her smile was so wide I thought that everyone in the park would be able to see by its light.

After dinner we gathered around people with guitars and mandolins, everyone singing and clapping to Grateful Dead songs. David was there, his arm wrapped around Barbara. Alfred squatted on the other side of the fire, his hands pantomiming the teeter-totter and how I fell off. Steven and Shelly, a "born again" couple, sat in their own little world. Larry hung back in the shadows with me, the flickering light from the fire only occasionally breaking the gloom around us. I had been drinking steadily all night.

Nicole, her guitar in the hands of someone else, said, "Look there!" and pointed behind me.

I turned around and saw the moose she was pointing to, its body hidden by high brush, and its head only barely discernible in the dark.

I again faced the fire and watched the smile on Michele's face grow, the fire dancing in her blue eyes, the breeze licking her dirty blond curls. A guy I didn't know dropped down next to her, pulling her to him and enfolding her with a meaty arm.

I wobbled to my feet and started for the moose.

"Hey, where are you going, Paul?" someone called out.

"Toilet's the other way!"

And as I got closer to the moose: "That thing'll kill you!"

"What a dumbshit."

Someone strummed a couple cords, and everyone began talking once again. I heard Michele's voice over the others, pitched high, but full, and disinterested in the moose and me.

I darted toward the brown lump absently eating dinner. The moose slowly raised her head, stopped chewing for a moment, and then sprang for deeper woods.

I followed, and lost her before the echoes of the picnic faded, but I kept running, tripping once, until I could hear absolutely nothing. Only then did I stop. In a clearing in the woods, the moon shone through the trees, illuminating piles of round moose droppings.

I sprinted around the park, keeping to the woods until I reached the bypass, and hitched a ride back to the spit.

At what was left of the City, I crossed the street and walked around the boat-filled harbor, through chaotic Winnebago Park, to the opposite beach on the spit. There were more rocks on this side, but I lay down anyway. I was at the End of the Road, and whatever energy had kept me going through the summer was suddenly gone. My feet were inches from the shoreline. The breeze raised goose bumps on my arms and the rocks jabbed into my back. The sky, as usual, was not black, but a dark purple, too light for stars, even though it was near midnight. The boardwalks, the restaurants, the fishing boats were behind me, out of sight. There was just the starless sky and the Kenai Range. The nearly full moon blazed down on the glaciers which split the white mountains across the bay into crests, like folded knees. The snow was completely melted from the ice fields, and bright blue ribbons streamed down them, as if a giant rake had scratched furrows there and the morning sun had poured into them.

In a whisper, I asked what lay, just beyond my grasp, in the heart of the mountains. But the only response was the gentle movement of the small waves and the sullen splashes of the returning salmon.

Breaking the Halibut

During the first shift of Glacier Crew, Alfred, an Aleut Native, told George and me that he'd guided for deer and grizzly hunters on Kodiak Island before coming to Homer, but his last time out, a hunter shot him in the arm because Alfred tried to hump his grandson during the night.

At the first break, Alfred unbuttoned his flannel shirt and showed us the scar.

"No, no," he said. "Don't hurt, no." He squeezed the worm-like bump on his bulging arm. "I tell old man before we leave city his gun too small. He shoot big bear with small gun and big bear come and ram small gun up his butt. I'm glad old man got crap in his ears."

The whole town knew George's story. He'd come from Seattle on his uncle's fishing boat, but as it pulled into Kachemak Bay, the Coast Guard boarded it and found a year-old marijuana cigarette wrapped in cellophane in George's army jacket.

"I thought my sister had swiped it and smoked it with her friends," he said. "It was in my pocket all along."

Even after impounding the boat and slapping on a one hundred thousand dollar fine, the government still said his uncle had to fire George, otherwise they'd tie up his boat for the whole summer. The petition signed by nearly every person in Homer didn't help. The government kept the boat through the halibut opening, bringing his uncle close to bankruptcy. He had to let George go.

Hell, I'd seen worse. Once in a bottling plant in Kansas City I worked with a guy who tried to loosen a chunk of debris that was holding up the line. When we pulled him from the sputtering machinery, all that was left of his arms was bits of pink flesh dripping from his splintered, ivory bones. And the last time I'd been in Alaska, nearly four years earlier, I saw two men fall to their deaths in Cook Inlet when they got too close to a flailing box trap full of King crab. Those men's fates were worse than George's, but at the time, I didn't feel sorry for them, just thought they were careless and forgot about it. But George got screwed. Not only that, he was determined to pay back the hundred thousand, plus the fifty thousand his uncle lost from missing the halibut opening. I couldn't figure him out. Who could?

And then it was my turn to tell George and Alfred how I came about to work a shit job like Glacier Crew. They sat across the table from me, waiting patiently. The most common lie I told about my past was the one where my wife took our newborn and ran off with a lawyer from Boise. The other migrant workers I met liked those types of stories best, where a woman is the cause of all your troubles. Men who find themselves bashing in pig skulls with a sledgehammer for a living, or bust their backs bailing hay, or carry around a pair of hands so dead with tendonitis they have to attach gutting knives to them with duct tape just to get through another shift of salmon season don't want to hear about reality.

But there was something about George's good intentions and Alfred's honesty that made me feel shitty about the lie I was going to feed them. So I didn't mention my marriage, or the laminated picture in my back pocket of the wife and child I had deserted in Pocatello five years earlier. Surely that'd be too much. Instead, I fed George and Alfred part of the truth. I unfolded the soiled map of Nepal I'd been carrying for a couple years and showed them the places I planned on seeing after the Alaskan salmon season.

"Hope to be there a while," I said. "Year or so. Make a trek to Everest."

Alfred rolled his lips and traced a finger along a red line I'd drawn through the Himalayas.

George nodded his head. Maybe it was me, but I think he expected more.

As I folded up the map, the slimers pounded up the stairs to the break room. Leo, our Russian supervisor, was in the lead.

"Alfred! George! Larry!" he said. "My Glacier Crew. I love my Glacier Crew." He was fat, his full bushy beard always tangled. He used to live in one of the Orthodox villages north of Homer, but left because he liked to smoke hashish and was always getting caught listening to the radio in the woods behind the church. Them Old Believers frown on that sort of thing.

"Time to work, work, work," Leo said.

We followed him down to the changing area and slid back into our yellow rain suits and blue gloves slippery with fish slime. During the first shift, Alfred started collecting the halibut eyeballs the fish guillotine had missed. He took a handful from his pocket and dropped them into some of the slimers' gloves hanging from pegs on the wall.

"Slimers need smiles," he said.

I laughed and turned to see if we got a chuckle out of George, but he was already wrapped up in his gear and jogging toward the Glacier room.

***

One half of the Glacier room was divided into two stalls. A little alley separated them. Leo drove the forklift and left totes of beheaded, gutted halibut at the open end of the first stall. Me, George and Alfred laid out a single flat layer of fish, green side up, stuffing each belly with ice, until the bottom of the first stall was covered with halibut linoleum, if you will. Then we dragged out the long black tube connected to the ice machine outside and blew a fine shower of snow over the fish, covering them with a two-inch layer. Leo brought more fish, and we repeated the process. We had to build this thing because after the twenty-four hour halibut opening, all the fishing boats packed into the Homer Spit harbor at once. It was necessary to preserve the biggest halibut in glaciers to give the slimers enough time to clean out the bloodlines of the smaller ones.

That first day, we worked six two and a half hour shifts. Alfred was certainly the strongest of us. While George and I had to strain together to pull the fish out of the iron tote, Alfred could just reach down, grab a tail with one hand, stuff his other into the hole where the head used to be, and with one beautiful heave fling a hundred and fifty pounder ten feet into the air.

George, however, worked the hardest. Even when there was a break in the action, George climbed down from the glacier, changed the bucket of iodine we used to sanitize our boots, shoveled away some fallen ice from Leo's path, then climbed back up to where Alfred and I dozed, using halibut as pillows. George's feet crunched the ice next to our heads as he filled a fish belly with even more ice and straightened the front row of the halibut layer in progress.

"Maybe I should grab the hose and blow some more ice up here," he said.

"Learn to pace yourself," I said. "Be plenty of work the next few days."

Alfred turned over on his side and pulled a halibut out of the row George had just straightened. He pried open its hole and scooped out the ice. A couple loosened fish slid down the incline and slapped against the top board holding in the glacier. One of the fish tumbled over the board and fell with a splat onto the concrete below.

"Tell you what, George," I said. "We'll get ourselves a drink at the Salty Dawg after work. My buy."

"I've got to work," he said.

"You're shittin' me. After fifteen hours here?"

"Repairing nets on the docks," he said.

Alfred ran his finger along the triangular gouge the guillotine had cut into the halibut, said the crack leading to the belly looked like a cunt.

"You put your thingee in here?" he asked. "How you put your thingee in here?"

***

One of the things I learned working such long shifts for days on end was how to get drunk quickly. The first night after Glacier Crew, Alfred and I pounded eight shots of tequila each in a half hour before we went stumbling out onto the docks looking for George. We didn't find him. I ended up losing Alfred somewhere in Winnebago Park, so I went back and drank more at the Salty Dawg. It must have been eleven by the time I was back in Tent City on the chunk of Homer Spit's beach Seward Fisheries leased out for its employees. The Northern sun was just about to dip behind the rolling hills freckled with pink and yellow wildflowers on the mainland when I crawled into my tent. Minutes later, I heard my wife calling me.

"Larry. Larry. Where are you?"

Two silhouettes were black against my green tent. One was shorter than the other and wore a dress that formed a sharp triangle, its edges undisturbed from the ocean breeze whistling between the other tents and rippling the walls of my own.

"Rose," I whispered. "Julie?"

I edged toward the flaps and looked out, but Tent City was quiet, its fires fallen to coals, the wind throwing clouds of sand into the empty air next to my tent.

Instead of shaking apart the vision in my mind, I dropped my head to the cool ground and tried to keep the two shadows motionless in my memory. It seemed that I had spent half my life with images floating in front of my eyes, images of my wife pacing our apartment floor, wondering, while I was out late at a bar playing poker, if I had turned myself into a bloody heap by slamming my truck into a tree. Images of her face imposed on a whore's, her eyes desperate when I touched her. Images of her walking to the store in the snow for baby formula because I couldn't resist a pool game after work. Images that dissolved, night after night, with another shot of whiskey, with a glance from a woman at the end of a bar, or with the sight of a third ace popping into my hand.

I turned my cheek away from the sand and waited for my wife's face to flash on the full moon. It happened sometimes. I watched the sky for a long time, noticed how the white moon seemed to anchor it, keeping the sky from flying away. Eventually, as the waves folded onto the beach, a purple band surrounding the moon expanded, soaking up the light blue sky, shoving away the scattered clouds, before it dropped like a curtain behind the snow-covered Kenai Mountains across the bay.

***

On the third day of Glacier Crew, George didn't show until noon. By that time, the second glacier was almost finished.

"Got to be on time," I said. "Not that it matters to me."

I had to talk to a woman from the ACLU," George said. "The fine has been reduced to ten thousand."

"Great," I said. "You hear that, Al?"

"Don't call me that," he said.

"Been talking about doing something," I said. "A party or something. This makes it better. Right, Alfred?"

"You like woman, we get you woman."

"Sure." George roped a halibut and dragged it toward the back wall.

I ran after him, falling a couple times on the ice, then stuffed his fish.

"Surely your uncle can absorb ten grand," I said.

George unroped the halibut and went back for another.

"The fine, and what he lost from missing the halibut opening, are my responsibilities, not his," he said.

"I don't get you," I said.

George looked like he was ready to say something, but just roped another fish. Leo drove in and lifted a tote of real monsters onto the first glacier.

"That one's done," I called.

"I love my Glacier Crew!" he said. "Up, up, up. Up to the ceiling we go!"

He backed away from the stall and stuffed a raspberry Zinger into his trap.

***

Alfred worked on the first glacier. Leo gave him the biggest and the fewest halibut. Between totes, Alfred either napped or watched George and me. Slowly, both glaciers drew closer to the ceiling and we began stooping, then crawling on our hands and knees to get the fish to the back of the stalls.

"I don't get you," I told George. "It's his damn boat. You plan on giving up living forever?"

"If I have to."

The ice had numbed my knees and elbows. Sweat inched down my back and hair was matted in strings to my forehead.

24

"Listen," I said. "You got friends here. Come to Nepal. Live like a king for five dollars a day."

"Run away and leave my uncle holding the bag," he said.

"Run away? Your uncle knows you can't raise that kind of cash. You're young. Don't you want to see places?"

I let go of my halibut, dropped to my side and leaned against the wall.

"Be like you, you mean?" George asked.

"Why not? Been all around the States. Been to every one except Hawaii. Plane stops there on the way to Asia. Been to Canada, too. All over. Seen lots of things."

George slid past me, fitted his halibut between two others.

"Wasn't much older than you when I went out on the road," I said. "Seen lots of things."

George passed me again on his way back to the pile of fish at the foot of the glacier.

"Slow down a minute, will you," I said. "Make me look bad."

George stopped and looked at me.

"Don't you ever get tired of the road?" he asked.

"Hell no," I said. "Can't think of a better life."

He shrugged and turned back around.

"Hold on," I called. "This old body needs a breather."

"Leo's coming with another tote," he said.

***

By the end of the next shift, all the fishing boats had been un-loaded, the halibut graded and beheaded, and, wiped out, me, George, and Alfred made it through the first stage of Glacier Crew. We fi-nished off the fifteen-hour day smashing apart frozen halibut, then filling boxes with them for shipment to the Lower Forty-Eight.

When we came back to the plant eight hours later, the Slime Line was ready for the glacier fish. Leo dumped an empty tote at the foot of the stall. We lifted out the top board and kicked the loose halibut down into the tote. As we dug deeper into the glacier and continued to remove the boards, the incline from the back wall to the front steepened. About a quarter the way in was a load of real monsters, maybe two hundred and fifty pounds each. I kicked and pushed at one. When the thing still wouldn't budge, I jumped on it. The halibut squirted out of its hold, rolled down the incline, taking me with it.

This was the first ride of what would become the Halibut Rodeo.

I shoved the fish down into the tote and climbed back up the glacier for another.

"Hey, George," I said. "Watch this."

I sat on a halibut, rocked back and forth, lifted my legs into the air, straightened my back, and slid down the glacier, riding the fish like a sled.

"Horsey, horsey!" Alfred said. He pounced on a fish and skidded down on his back, losing his mount midway. I jumped on the halibut, tied my tugging rope around the tail as fast as I could, and then pranced around it, swinging my cap in the air.

"King of the Rodeo," I said. "Let's take a bow, Alfred. Come on, George."

"Leo will shit if he sees you," George said.

But we always heard the forklift long before it reached the Glacier room.

The course got longer and faster as Alfred and I rode the topmost halibut down and George pulled out the fish in the middle and at the foot of the glacier.

Considering his size, Alfred rode the best he could. His feet always seemed to drop before he picked up speed. He either came to a standstill halfway down or flipped over.

"Come on, George," I said. "I need someone to race."

At the top of the glacier, I found a nice flexible mount. For maximum speed, I tied a rope around the tail and held the rope over my shoulder. I put the fingers of my other hand into the windpipe and clutched the front part of the fish between my uplifted legs. With just the midsection of the fish touching the ice, I soared down the glacier, blowing past George and Alfred, the rush knocking off my cap, ice ricocheting off my tingling cheeks, my stomach contracting. And when I hit bottom I pulled hard on the rope, swinging the fish around, sending a fine spray of ice over the wall and into the tote below.

"Beat that," I told George, trudging back up to him. "You got to try. Besides, it's efficient too. Look how quickly the glacier's shrinking."

George sighed and toed a fish.

"It's easy," I said.

He dropped on top of the halibut, rode it as if body surfing.

"All right, George!" Alfred and I yelled.

George ran back up the glacier and took one down rodeo-style.

"Not bad for a young cowpoke," I said.

"This is nuts," he said.

We had races and we all promised to get together after work for a barbecue and to listen to Country-Western tapes. By the end of the fourth shift, the foot of the glacier was only a few layers of fish high. The top of an empty tote rose six inches or so above the remaining boards.

Alfred and I sat in the ice while George cleared a trail all the way to the back wall. We hadn't taken that many fish from the back rows yet, so when George searched through the ice for the perfect mount he had to crawl to do it. When he found a fish he was happy with, he pulled it into position, tied his rope around the tail, turned his baseball cap around, and put his fingers into the windpipe.

I scrambled halfway up the glacier. We had worn a groove in the ice; it was slick and shiny. I looked up and saw George sitting on his fish, waiting for my signal. He didn't look too much different than me, I supposed: same black Wellingtons, a baseball cap, and the yellow rain suit that turned him into a giant banana.

I reached down and touched the smooth ice. I looked up again. George seemed even higher, the course steeper.

"Y'all hang on tight, y'hear?" I said.

George inched forward.

"Ready," he said.

I swung my arm. George pushed out with his legs, and then lifted them.

"Yeeeehawwwww!" he yelled.

He hit the lip of the steepest drop, stopping at the edge for a split second, and then through an icy mist he careened down the glacier.

Grinning wide, his ass lifted inches off the fish, back straight, toes pointed toward the ceiling.

Out of the corner of my eye I spotted the huge, green halibut lightly dusted with ice at the bottom of the drop.

"George!"

I lunged for the yellow blur streaking past me, but I missed. When George hit the halibut's back, he jettisoned forward, catapulting over the top board and off the glacier. He managed to drop his legs at the last moment, but his knees and his halibut still crashed into the lip of the iron tote, and he barreled in head first, out of sight.

***

"What the hell is this?" I asked no one in particular. "I can always get a ride off the Spit."

Alfred and I had been walking twenty minutes, past the harbor, the halibut charters and the sourdough bakeries. A guy on the radio once said that Homer was as far as you could go without a passport. He's right, in a way. The westernmost highway in North America ends at the tip of Homer Spit, only about a hundred yards from Seward Fisheries. It's no wonder so many migrant workers like me end up there. Seems to be the last place to go. Alfred and I were headed in the opposite direction, away from the end of the road, back towards town to visit George in the hospital. He had a broken shoulder and his face was messed up.

I kept my thumb in the air, but Alfred didn't bother. He'd saunter down the embankment and examine a rock, a dropped fishing lure, a clamshell.

"You could help, you know."

"They don't trust Natives," he said.

"That's ridiculous," I said. But, after a pick-up with an empty bed sped past, I gave up and we walked along the beach.

Homer Spit is five miles long and, in places, only a few hundred yards wide. There are no trees to stop the wind rolling in from the Pacific. By the time we reached the mainland, I couldn't stop shivering and my skin was tight with goose bumps. The sun had slipped behind the hills outside of town, and once again that strange shade of purple washed the sky. I looked at the moon for my wife's face. Nothing. The moon was no longer full. A sliver was missing, as if someone had pared it with a knife.

"Wish we had something to take George," I said.

"We get something," Alfred said. "Big, fancy chicken. Kind you don't eat."

Alfred's "big fancy chicken" was a peacock.

We walked up the Homer by-pass and into the woods behind the old high school. Well-worn paths wound around the trees and their exposed roots. What looked like an old obstacle course was spread across the edge of the woods nearest the school. Ropes, tires, pulleys and wire were strung above us in the trees.

"Strange place for a chicken," I said.

Five minutes into the woods, Alfred stopped and we left the path. The trees opened up and we crouched down in front of a domed cage. I heard a rustle inside of a small wooden house on the far side of the cage, and then out jumped the peacock, tail feathers down, its fluorescent greenish-blue coat capturing shards of moonlight.

Alfred circled towards the door of the cage and jiggled the latch. As he opened the door, a shadow behind him moved. I heard a click.

"Son of a bitch!" someone yelled. An explosion rocked the air and the branch above me shattered in a rain of leaves and splinters. The peacock let loose with an ear-piercing scream.

I jumped and ran, tripping over a root and landing hard on my knee. Alfred pulled me up by the hood of my jacket and propelled me forward.

Just a few minutes run from the cage, Alfred dropped behind a fallen tree.

"Rest later," I hissed.

"He don't follow."

I started to limp away, but then turned back around.

"Let's go get a drink," I said.

"Be dark enough soon to go get chicken," Alfred said.

I sat next to him and sighed. I was tired of running.

"What's he going to do with a damn peacock," I said.

Alfred shrugged.

"You think it's our fault, don't you?" I said. "Our fault he's busted up. That's bullshit, man. He should've known how fast he was going."

Alfred probably wasn't convinced of that. I know I wasn't. He took two Hershey bars out of his pocket and handed me one.

"He's going to lose his job at Sew-Fish, isn't he?" I asked.

"No job for one-handed guys," Alfred said.

"Think we can get him work somewhere?"

"Maybe."

"Say, Alfred," I said. "You ever been to Nepal?"

He shook his head. I took out my map.

"Ever want to?" I asked.

He shook his head again.

"Yeah," I said. I dropped the map and reached into my back pocket for the laminated picture of my family.

I cupped the picture in my hand. Every time I looked at it, it seemed as if the colors had faded, just a little, from the time before. I knew that someday all the color would be gone, leaked out from underneath the lamination. Left behind would be only degrees of black and white, my wife and child only shadows.

"Going to show this to George when you and I take him the peacock." I handed the picture to Alfred.

"That's my wife, Julie, and my baby girl, Rose. Must be about six now."

"Pretty girls," he said, handing back the picture.

"Yeah," I said. "I bet they are."

I dropped the picture into my breast pocket and patted it. The image burned in my memory, I leaned back against the tree and waited for the dark.

The Prince of Kodiak

Ten days before he picked up Charlie Connel by the belt loop and flannel collar and tossed him through the front window of the Salty Dawg Saloon, Alfred was slinging halibut on case-up crew and beginning to wonder if he was gay after all. He and Steven Parker were in back of a semi-trailer with a basket full of one hundred pounders and up, all gutted and frozen, and ready for shipment to the Lower Forty-Eight. The fish had to be stacked in the trailer like bricks, but front to tail so that they remained balanced until there was a sturdy enough wall to hold in the halibut that Alfred and Steven heaved over and behind it. Alfred had just lifted a hundred and fifty pounder from the basket when something began to turn and twist in his gut.

At first Alfred wondered if he was having a heart attack. Steven had been droning on about the miracles in the New Testament, saying how Joseph Campbell was wrong when he assumed that the Holy Virgin's ascension into heaven was simply metaphor. Alfred, an Aleut Native, had no idea what he was talking about, so while he lifted fish from the basket, tossed them over his shoulder and behind the halibut wall, he ignored Steven and looked down the long, dark tunnel of the trailer to where the rest of case-up crew was framed in a square of yellow light, bagging the smaller halibut for fresh shipment.

The pain hit Alfred when Anneke walked into the square of yellow to talk to the forklift driver. Like all the Russian women working at the plant, she wore a long printed skirt, a white blouse with puffed sleeves, and a bandanna to keep her hair pulled back tight behind her ears. Alfred held his burning chest and examined her white skin, her sharp cheekbones, and the eyes that looked too large for her face. She was small and delicate, and the way her skirt sashayed against her rubber boots when she walked made Alfred's face burn and his body ache.

When Alfred believed that his mind couldn't cope with what was going on in front of him, or even inside of him, he tended to resort to tossing his whole body into the situation, hoping that his sheer physical size would do the talking for him. So he dropped the fish he was holding and sifted through the rest until he found the biggest one. He raised the whole two hundred pounds of it above his head, his mind and straining muscles momentarily becoming one and, with all his might, pitched the fish into the back of the trailer. It crashed into the wall and sent a clap of thunder, like tearing metal, past him and Steven and into the plant. The rest of the case-up crew, including Anneke, looked up curiously before going back to stuffing halibut into plastic bags.

"Take it easy there, big guy," Steven said.

With his small black eyes, and from his six foot six height, Alfred peered down at Steven, flexed his muscles and grunted.

"The disciples were fishermen," Steven said. "In Christ's day the fishermen were the strongest, the wrestlers of the first century. Even Saviors need bodyguards. Christ knew what he was doing. You, Alfred, could be such a fisherman."

"You talk with riddles," Alfred said.

He reached down for another fish. Anneke fluttered in the distance. The pain shot back into his gut. He remained motionless, his body bent into the metal basket.

Instead of thinking through his decisions, Alfred tended to react to situations. But as he hung over the basket, something Steven had said hours before came back to him. He eased himself prone and backed against the side wall of the trailer. Even though he never smoked, he suddenly had the taste for a cigarette. Detectives in movies, he recalled, always seemed to smoke as they leaned against a rain-soaked building, the clues in their minds unscrambling toward a logical motive.

"In old book," Alfred said, "Jews are chosen people. In new book, Christians are chosen people."

"Yes," Steven said. "Please continue."

"Why is this?" Alfred asked.

"Very interesting question, Alfred." Steven took off his Red Sox cap and combed back his hair with his fingers. "Because Alfred," he answered, pointing two fingers at him like a pair of six shooters. "Because God made a mistake."

"God make mistake?"

"In ways, He is just like us."

Back in the plant, Anneke diligently bagged halibut. The wrenching returned, but now, maybe because Alfred was used to it, the throbbing didn't seem so painful.

Alfred never actually thought of being gay, just accepted it after he felt compelled to hump a fifteen year old boy on Kodiak Island while he was guiding grizzly bear hunters. The boy's grandfather had caught Alfred in the act and shot him in the arm. Alfred left the island–his family, his Aleut heritage–to start a new life in Homer. Whatever possessed him to advance on the boy disappeared as soon as he left home.

Alfred looked again at Anneke and scratched his ear. He pictured himself hopping over the basket of fish, scooping up her fragile body into his callused hands, and holding her to the sunlight as if she were a porcelain doll.

"God make mistake," he said.

During the next ten days, Alfred could think only of Anneke. He pushed Charlie Connel and his two-year old war with him far back into his mind. But during those ten days, Alfred never said a word to Anneke. He simply positioned himself near her at every possibility. When break was called, he jumped over the basket in the trailer and followed her up to the break room. When they ate, he sat at the table opposite her, in plain view, so she could see his expressionless face. When it was time to go home, he clocked out before she did so he could be at the door, casually skipping stones on the gravel and clamshell lot as she and Rachel, the friend she rode with, headed for their red jeep.

Alfred wondered if her friend wasn't the Rachel, the Russian woman who was found wandering around the beach drunk one early morning the summer before, her bright skirt and blouse matted with mud, hair tangled and clotted with small sea shells. Over her shoulder she carried the thirty-pound King salmon she had supposedly dragged out of the Kachemak Bay shallows with her bare hands and beat dead with a piece of drift wood. That had caused quite a stir in Red'kin, the village of Russian Old Believers north of Homer. No way would the village Elders accept Alfred, but maybe, like Rachel, Anneke didn't care much for all the rules of her village.

At first, Anneke didn't seem to notice Alfred's attentions. But on the fifth day, as they walked up to the break room, she turned on Alfred and sneered. The sneering continued for two days. Then for two more days she simply looked at him with the same expressionless face he had for her. On the tenth, Anneke and Rachel paused in the parking lot. They watched Alfred skip stones for a moment, and then piled into the jeep giggling.

Alfred doubled over and held the newest knot in his chest.

***

The halibut season ended. The Salty Dawg Saloon grew packed with Spit Rats from Seward Fisheries and fishermen getting their last few good drunks in before the salmon season hit hard. Alfred shuffled through the sawdust and squeezed in at the bar. Bart the barman set him up with his usual shot of tequila and nodded toward the end of the bar. Charlie was there, leaning over a bottle of Chinook ale, trying to get a fix on Alfred.

"Step easy, son," Bart said. "For some damn reason ol' Charlie's got quite a lot of support around here."

The problem was, Alfred never know who was against him and who was indifferent. He once let it be known, through lips numb with tequila, what had happened back on Kodiak. Most of the men who were at the Salty Dawg that night probably didn't remember the confession in the morning. Others, in their new-found alcoholic camaraderie with Alfred shrugged, and said, "Hell, everyone has their hobbies. Now pass that bottle." These were the ones who woke up the next day to the sobering rays of the morning sun and recalled that the big ass Native wasn't exactly "normal." At least that's the way Alfred heard it. There weren't many secrets in a small town like Homer.

Since Alfred first stepped into the Salty Dawg, Charlie Connel shied away from him. Alfred could tell when someone was threatened by his size. The night after Alfred's confession, Charlie sat in a corner of the saloon, buying rounds for some of the same men Alfred had confessed to. They whispered at the table, shooting glances at Alfred who nursed a tequila at the bar.

To make matters worse, Alfred and Larry Bond, a migrant worker from Idaho, had once stolen Charlie's peacock from its cage in his back yard, then gave it to a work mate who was laid up in the hospital. Alfred didn't know it was Charlie's. He wished Larry were with him now. He had been the closest thing to a friend Alfred had in Homer, but he'd gone back to Pocatello in search of the family he had deserted.

"Bart," Alfred said. "Another ale for Charlie."

The men beside Alfred turned their heads sharply and squinted. Bart poured Alfred another shot.

"You up to something I should know about, son?"

"An ale for Charlie," Alfred said.

Bart raised his eyebrows and popped open a bottle of Chinook.

Alfred didn't look down the bar for Charlie's response, just drank his tequila and imagined him first ignoring the bottle when he found out who sent it, then grabbing it like it was a trophy, as if Alfred was giving up the fight.

And he would be right. Over the past ten days Alfred felt something inside begin to soften. Not only did he want acceptance from Anneke, but from the people of Homer as well, including Charlie. This was his home. Who knows, maybe he'd have kids someday. People thought that because Alfred was quiet, he was mean. But actually, Alfred felt ashamed because he wasn't book smart, didn't even graduate from high school. He was too uncomfortable to talk much. Maybe if he convinced Charlie that he was no threat, others in Homer would fall into place.

"What's the big idea?"

Alfred turned and looked down at the man he had been feuding with for the past two years. Charlie strained his neck to meet Alfred's eyes, then took a quick drink of his Chinook and wiped his brow. At the nearest tables, men and their dates watched carefully. The serious drinkers at the bar kept their backs straight, but bent their necks to keep an eye out for action.

"What's this?" Charlie asked, holding up his bottle.

He spit when he talked. Every time a woman dumped Charlie, Bart made a point to slip on his rain slicker, more for effect than defense, as Charlie always got pissed drunk during those times, and, as custom demanded, spilled his guts at the bar, and his saliva on Bart. Charlie never did see the bright yellow coat as a sign of ridicule; instead, between the breaths of his monologues, his eyes darted toward the ceiling in expectation, Alfred supposed, of dripping leaks.

"Free ale," Alfred said.

"What the hell for," Charlie said. "We ain't friends." His lips curled, baring teeth yellowed with hand-rolled cigarettes. Others were so black that Alfred couldn't see them at all in the darkness of the Salty Dawg.

"No more fighting," Alfred said.

"Is that a fact," Charlie said. "Who says?"

Alfred waved Bart over and tipped his head toward Charlie. Bart placed another sweating bottle of Chinook on the bar.

"Look," Charlie said. He held up his hand and downed the rest of his beer. "This won't cut it." He placed the empty on the bar and picked up the other bottle.

"First we quit fighting for no damn reason, then you start buying me beers? Hell, you're, well, you know, one of them." He chugged his beer and slammed the empty bottle on the bar.

"I got a reputation to uphold," Charlie said, turning to walk away.

Alfred's hand clamped down on Charlie's shoulder. The saloon fell silent.

"Easy, son," Bart said.

Charlie had never actually confronted Alfred physically, and even when he could swing men over to his side with a free drink, they never put themselves in front of Alfred. They did their fighting by whispering behind Alfred's back and spreading rumors about him. They always made themselves scarce when it looked as though something serious was about to erupt.

Charlie's stiffened shoulder relaxed under Alfred's grasp.

"Well, what about my damn peacock?" Charlie said loudly enough for the whole saloon to hear.

"You got fancy chicken back." Alfred let go of his grip.

Charlie popped his neck and straightened the collar of his flannel shirt.

"What the hell does that matter," he said loudly. "She ain't been the same since you stole her. Always screaming."

Alfred didn't have a reply for that. He turned back to the bar.

"You ruined that poor thing's life," Charlie continued. "Never be the same. Never."

"Go on back to your place, Connel," Bart said. "Here, son." He poured Alfred another shot. "You tried, and that takes a big man. But some just can't be pleased."

Alfred drank his tequila and scanned the saloon. In the crowd, toward the back, he swore he saw Steven Parker. For a moment, he felt more comfortable, knowing there was another friendly face, besides Bart's, around. But he couldn't find him again. Besides, Steven had never been in the Salty Dawg before. Why would he show up now and not be home with his wife? His god wouldn't approve.

Meanwhile, Charlie had sat down at the table near the Kiss pinball machine.

"Another ale," Alfred said.

Bart leaned across the bar.

"Son, you know what you're doing?"

The men next to Alfred leaned closer to the conversation.

"Mind your own beeswax," Bart told them.

"Another ale," Alfred repeated.

Bart sighed and popped open another bottle.

"You got nothing to prove," he said.

Two other men sat at Charlie's table. When Alfred approached, they shoved their chairs back and eased away. Charlie was preoccupied with a girl playing the pinball machine. His head swung back and forth in time with her hips. He had a reputation for grabbing any curve that walked past his bar stool. Even after being knocked unconscious by Judith, a tall redhead from Holland who challenged all to matches of arm wrestling, a shot of vodka for the winner, Charlie continued his groping, just kept to the underage girls who snuck in to play pinball.

"Would you lookie there," he said, mesmerized.

Alfred placed the bottle on the table. Charlie didn't turn around until a sudden silence dropped on the saloon. Alfred sat down, the chair creaking beneath his weight.

"What the hell do you want from me," Charlie said. "Can't you see I'm busy?"

"No more fighting," Alfred said.

Charlie took a swig of the beer. "What the hell's the matter with you, anyway?" He looked again at the swaying hips. "Look at that move. Hell, why would you care.'

Alfred had to pin his hands between legs and chair to keep from reaching up and tearing his own hair out. The right words wouldn't form in his mouth. In his old village, all disputes could be settled with a beer, or the lending of a helping hand to repair a broken fence or roof. Charlie was different, however, and all Alfred could think to do was to keep feeding him liquor, to find the companionship that was sometimes found at the bottom of an empty bottle.

"Another ale?" Alfred asked.

"Nah."

The girl playing pinball kicked the machine before walking away.

She was quickly replaced by another. Alfred blinked. For a split second, he thought she was Anneke. She stood the same height and carried the same sharp cheekbones. He looked toward the front window, wondering if the red jeep was parked outside.

"Now, we're talking." Charlie shifted to the edge of his seat, bringing him just inches from the girl's backside. She was too involved in her game to notice.

A small alarm ringed in Alfred's chest. He knew the girl wasn't Anneke, but the resemblance was startling, she was just younger, not older than sixteen.

"I'm sorry about fancy chicken," he announced.

Charlie cocked his head and looked at him. "Yeah," he said. "Well, maybe you could spring for a peacock psychiatrist, eh?" He laughed and slapped the table.

Heat rose to Alfred's cheeks. He felt the eyes in the Salty Dawg boring in on him. He didn't know what was so funny.

Charlie stood behind the girl. Before that night, Alfred had never even looked twice when Charlie moved in on the girls, yet tonight Alfred's heart beat faster and beads of sweat rolled down his neck.

"No," he murmured, too faintly for anyone to hear.

Charlie was right up on the girl now, close enough to where Bart wouldn't be able to see what he was about to do. The girl didn't notice until Charlie's hand was between her legs. Then he squeezed.

Speechless, the girl jumped. She backed away from Charlie slowly, her nostrils flaring, the color drained from her face. Tears pooled in the corner of her wide eyes and her arms trembled.

Alfred's chest heaved, and his breath burned his nostrils. He clenched his fists and placed them quietly on the table.

When Charlie began to laugh, the girl sprang toward the door. The laughter was thin and tinny in Alfred's ears. He saw Bart moving to the end of the bar.

But Alfred reached Charlie first. He grabbed him by his belt and collar, and as if Alfred was back in the trailer slinging halibut, he lifted him over his head, took five steps toward the front window and heaved him forward, Charlie screaming and flaying his arms the whole time. Charlie flew through a shower of glass shards and wooden splinters, landing in the gravel and clamshells outside; the impact threw up a thick cloud of gray dust.

The ocean wind immediately blasted into the Salty Dawg, blowing Alfred's long black hair behind him. The exertion had settled his heart. He turned and met fifty astonished faces. And sure enough, Steven's was among them. Alfred wanted to step toward him, wanted some kind of reassurance, but he couldn't read the other man's blank expression.

Bart leant against the bar. His face was down. He wouldn't meet Alfred's eyes.

Still silent, the patrons raised their chins, trying to glance out the window. Nothing stirred out there. Alfred was about to look out, but was suddenly afraid. What about the girl, he wanted to ask.

He fumbled in his pockets for his drink money and laid a twenty on the bar.

"Sorry," he mumbled, then ducked out of the Salty Dawg, careful not to look at the crumpled man just outside the window.

***

More than usual, the Spit Rats, the fair weather clam hunters, fishermen, both professional and amateur, sourdough bakers and assorted transients sped up their pace when Alfred walked by, dropped their gazes to the road, stepped into a bait shop or corner store. Alfred was accustomed to being avoided. Just being a Native was a strike against him. He was probably the only person in town who could never hitch a ride on or off five mile long Homer Spit. He was used to that, and didn't really mind waking up two hours before starting time to walk from his one room cabin behind McDonald's to Seward Fisheries at the tip of the Spit. Never before, however, did the citizens of Homer go to such lengths to avoid him.

Luckily, Alfred's supervisor didn't care about what happened outside the plant. Salmon season had begun, and Alfred became an Ice Pilot. He no longer worked with Steven. But as an Ice Pilot, he was able to stretch his muscles by shoveling ten or twelve tons of ice every two hours, and there was plenty of lag time for him to sit back and watch Anneke, cleaning fish over on the Slime-Line, not more than twenty feet away. As he watched her work now, however, he set the frightened face of the girl Charlie had manhandled right next to Anneke's and checked for resemblances. He discovered a common frailty, and it became important to place her on a pedestal, to keep her high and away from the Charlies in the world, while he stood guard underneath.

Four days after the Salty Dawg incident, Alfred swallowed his fear and sat down across from Anneke during dinner break. He heard a chair scrape, saw a departing shadow, but he kept himself too engrossed with the halibut and steak in front of him, too nervous to even look at the eyes which had already met his own many times before in the last two weeks, and reluctant to find out she had left as soon as he sat down.

"You are big, silly son of bitch." Anneke's accent was strong. "Bitch" sounded like "beech." Alfred took comfort in that. He looked up. Rachel was the one who had left the table.

"You are pretty dresser," he said.

Anneke frowned.

"I don't like this," she said, fingering her skirt. "Me, I like jeans. Like yours. In village, they tell us do this, do that. No jeans." She sighed.

Alfred nodded, doing little justice to the leaps his heart was making in his chest.

***

After work, Alfred spent an hour in a cold drizzle across the street from the Salty Dawg. The red jeep had passed him four times, once slowing down in front of him. When he saw the jeep, and imagined who was in it, Homer and its people lost importance. But the feeling didn't last when he thought about the many hours he had spent under the saloon's rotting beams, leaning back against walls carved with names, stick figures and silent wishes. The Salty Dawg was the place of closest contact between him and the rest of Homer. Rejected there, work or not, and he would be rejected completely from the town. Accepted there, maybe Anneke would take even greater notice of him, see he was not threatening in the least.

Alfred crossed the street. The Salty Dawg was actually an old lighthouse and still sent its circling beam across Kachemak Bay. Alfred stopped at the boarded up window, looked up at the rain dropping through the searchlight, and then stepped inside.

Because there was no window, the saloon was even darker than usual, but the patrons immediately recognized Alfred and ceased talking long enough for him to lumber up to the bar.

"Son," Bart said, shaking his head. "This is a bad idea. Connel is too smart to bring in the police, but don't push it."

"I must pay for window." Alfred dropped three one hundred dollars bills on the bar.

41

Mark Lewandowski

"Now, son. You know I like you." Bart hesitated before scooping up the money. "You're a good customer, never have tabs like some of these jokers in here. And that body of yours will stop just about any type of fight getting ready to fire up, but people have been talking. A lot are afraid of you these days."

"No more fighting." Alfred placed two dollars on the bar.

"Just one." Bart poured Alfred his tequila. "Then you get lost for a while. Let things cool down."

"Well, look who's here." Charlie had snuck up behind Alfred.

"Hell, Connel," Bart said. "I thought you were gone for the night."

"An ale," Alfred said to Bart.

"I don't want your charity," Charlie said. "I want your faggot ass out of town."

"You want trouble, Connel," Bart said. "Take it outside."

Alfred turned. Charlie was holding both his hands in the air, as if he couldn't move them. Both were wrapped up to the shoulder with white bandages. His left forearm was much thicker than the right. Alfred assumed there was a cast beneath the wrappings. Smaller strips of bandages crisscrossed his face and neck and one eye was black.

"What you call me?" Alfred asked.

"I said I want you out of this town. You ain't wanted here." Charlie looked over his shoulder. Two men Alfred had never seen before stood, with arms crossed, on either side of the pinball machine. Alfred remembered the girl who, just a few nights earlier, had stood in the place between the two men. Anger bubbled in his throat.

Alfred stared down the two men.

"Are you leaving?" Charlie asked.

Alfred puffed out his chest and squinted. One of the men shuffled his feet and turned toward the pinball machine, but the other took a step forward.

"Hell, Charlie," he said. "He's not so big."

"Look again," said a familiar voice from a dark corner of the Salty Dawg. A moment later, Steven stepped forward into the gloomy light and nodded to Alfred.

"God bless you," he said.

The voice seemed to have a magical effect on the crowd; all took their attention away from what they were doing and rested their eyes on the man who had stepped out of the darkness to bless Alfred.

"Thank you," Alfred replied.

The people in the saloon murmured and looked around at one another, then toward Alfred, then Steven, and finally, they all brought their gazed back to Charlie.

"You hear me?" Charlie asked Alfred, his voice cracking on the last word.

The men sitting in the center of the saloon cleared a circle by pushing their tables and chairs back.

"That's not going to be necessary!" Bart said. "I'm pleading with you, son."

"No more fighting," Alfred shouted, his fists clenched.

"All you got to do is leave," Charlie said.

Alfred was ready to. Even though it seemed as if the people of Homer were giving him plenty of room to have it out, once and for all, with Charlie, he was ready to leave that saloon forever, to get rid of the hatred that would not let his soul rest, to leave it behind in the sawdust, the sticky spills and the fishy smells of the Salty Dawg. He would have if, at the moment Charlie was taking his stand, Anneke and Rachel, with nervous smiles and dancing eyes, had not wandered into the doorway of the saloon. All Charlie did was look in their direction, a simple glance anyone would have given a sneeze during a speech, or to a moose on the side of the road, to any momentary distraction.

Alfred looked quickly from the girls, to Charlie, and then to Steven. His work-mate raised an eyebrow, pointed two fingers at him, and mouthed the word "bodyguard."

That's all it took for Alfred. The anger snapped in his mouth. He grabbed hold of Charlie Connel by belt loop and collar, raised him above his head, took three steps forward and slammed the screaming man into the plywood holding back the ocean wind. Charlie bounced off the boards, landed squarely on a table, bursting it into kindling, sending its occupants crashing into the people seated next to them, beer, ice and whisky flying through the air. One glass shattered into a storm of slivers right in front of the man who had stepped forward from the pinball machine; he stepped back into the shadows.

"He's crazy!" Charlie whimpered, face red and wet, and holding his arm. "Absolutely crazy." He was splayed out on the floor, surrounded by unraveling bandages and white chunks and dust from his cracked open cast.

"I like girls," Alfred said. "You don't." He turned toward the door, but Anneke and Rachel were gone. He wondered if they had really been there.

"What the hell does that mean? You're nuts," Charlie looked for his support near the pinball machine, but it was long gone.

No one moved for a moment. Alfred watched Charlie search the faces around him imploringly, but all he saw were downcast eyes, expressions of sadness and pity, looking down at the broken statue of a man in front of them. Soon after, the witnesses to the event went back to their drinks and their own problems.

After he left the Salty Dawg that night, Alfred stopped first at his cabin for his newest looking pair of jeans before walking the three hours to the Russian village. By then, dawn was about to break and the village was fast asleep. Huddling against a tree for warmth, he slept a little and waited for the red jeep to pull away from the white, wooden houses with bright green and yellow trim.

At 7:30, the jeep appeared on the dirt road leading to Homer. Alfred sprang up and tore through the trees. When he reached the woods' edge, he leapt into the road. The jeep swerved away from him and nearly slid into the ditch on the side of the road.

Anneke rolled down her window, anger creasing her face.

"You big silly son of bitch," she said. "Always crashing and smashing."

"Sorry," Alfred said. "Long walk to work."

He held the jeans in front of him.

Anneke's mouth opened in an "O." She hopped out of the jeep.

"Yes," Rachel said from behind the wheel. "Who cares if we are late?"

Anneke took the jeans and held them against herself; they came up to her chin.

"Big and silly," she said. "Lots of room, yes?" Still holding the jeans with one hand, she pushed back the front seat.

"Okay, crazy person," she said. "Get in."

Alfred grinned and climbed into the back seat.

King Salmon

I'm not the boy's sponsor, but because I'm the oldest in the group and been going to the meetings longer than anyone else, I can't help but grow concerned when someone suddenly stops showing up. He'd been coming to meetings three, four times a week for the past year. My first thought was that he started drinking again. That's always my first thought. I still was afraid of that after he called me at home and invited me over for supper and a Vikings game. We weren't friends of any kind, and even though everyone who meets regularly has my home number, people usually don't call, so I went out to his complex on the edge of Sioux Falls with reluctance. This had all the earmarks of a confession.

He didn't say much during the first half, just plied me with chips and dip. During commercials, while he fussed with the grill, I looked around his apartment: the freshly painted walls, the magazines neatly stacked and the pictures recently dusted. He even had plants. Not only did this hardly seem the abode of someone recently coming off a bender, I'd have to say he was either expecting a woman, or was a bit effeminate himself. He never struck me that way.

By halftime the Vikes were down seventeen-zip. He set our plates on a brand new coffee table. He'd grilled these monster salmon steaks, each about three inches thick. We tore into them. I didn't even notice there was a potato on the plate until that steak was reduced to bone. I ate like there was no tomorrow; like that fish was the last of its kind in the whole ocean.

"That's a fish," I said, sitting back and patting my belly. "Where'd you get something like that?"

"Alaska," he said.

I let it sink in. Is that where he was?

He zapped the sound on the television.

"You want to hear about it?" he asked.

"Sure," I said. "You went up there on vacation? Never been there myself. Heard it was pretty. I bet you got some pictures to show."

"I wasn't there on any vacation," he said. "I went up there to recti-fy a wrong."

He lit up a cigarette and offered me his pack.

"Thanks," I said.

"A terrible wrong," he said. "Back when."

"All right then," I said. "Take your time."

The boy took one big draw on his butt and then let loose.

Nearly four thousand miles. I drove it in five days. It's crazy, really. I hadn't seen or heard from Michele in two years, but I had an engagement ring in my pocket and I was determined to get it on her finger. All I knew about her whereabouts was the town and the joint she worked for: "Homer" and "Seward Fisheries." Homer's a small town. Finding her was easy. The first guy I came across outside Seward Fisheries, some big Eskimo name of Alfred, told me that, come nine o'clock, I'd find Michele at the Salty Dawg Saloon.

I had to interrupt: "What kind of name is that? Sounds made up."

"That's what I thought," he continued, "but there you have it. I hadn't been in a bar since I went cold turkey. That's the last place I wanted to confront Michele. I was a different person back when we were together, you know."

I nodded.

I was nervous. Back in the old days I'd never just walk up to some girl in a bar unless I had at least a little buzz going. I was toasted the night I'd met Michele at the Alcove. Remember that place? Over three years ago. Jesus. I'd just barged into the Alcove and there she was, dressed for summer in cut-offs and one of those tight, elastic halter top things. All tall and slender, she was. I marched straight up to her and said something like, "This is it. I'm not going any further. No further into this bar or further into life unless you're with me."

She didn't even blink.

"Talk to me some more like that," she said in this quirky voice, all sing-song, you might say. Like she's talking through a clarinet or something. By the number of shot glasses lined up in front of her I knew she had to hold onto something to keep from falling on her ass.

So I fed her some more liquor, and she fed me some more, and soon we were back in my brother's apartment banging away. We didn't come up for air for two days. This time around I thought I'd try it the same way, just no liquor. But nine o'clock was a while away yet. I found a shack of a restaurant and had clam chowder and sourdough bread, then sat there with a Coke until it was too warm to drink. After, I messed with the tackle box I'd picked up in Whitehorse, took some walks on the beach, etc. all the way to nine. I'd just burst in, I thought, act like I owned the place, like there was nothing unusual about me being there. I'd just march up to wherever she was and lay down the ring.

It didn't turn out so easy. I saw her as soon as I walked in. She was at the bar. Her blond hair was a mess of curls on her broad shoulders. Underneath was a red flannel shirt that'd seen better days. Then below was a pair of torn jeans worn white at the butt. She smoked a cigarette that looked like a joint and arched her neck to let out the smoke. She didn't notice me being nervous as shit in the doorway. Thank God for that. I needed the second. I felt stupid in front of her beauty, by my own passion, by the sudden flood of memories that crashed on me. Not the patches of scenes I'd been drumming up the past two years, but real life, right there, the smoke in the air, the beer on the tables, the loud music, all that talking, and Michele, like we'd never left each other, like all those dreams of her and all my changes were just some kind of string to follow. And it was tied to the door handle of the Salty Dawg. I tugged it open and there it was, like an empty spool, my old life, all the bad shit stripped away to leave Michele. That was everything, wasn't it?"

I nodded and stamped out my smoke.

An empty shot glass was in front of her, just one, and next to that a pack of Marlboro Reds; one was still in the ashtray snaking out smoke. I was shaking like crazy, but managed to light my own cigarette.

"This is it," I said, moving in on her. "I'm not going any further." I paused then for drama, or so I like to think; my hands trembled so much I dropped my cigarette.

"Jesus shit," Michele said, not at all in the sing-song voice I remembered. She always talked sing-song, whether she was really pissed off or happy as hell. I never could tell what mood she was in.

"Jesus ate shit. I didn't hear that," she went on, and just like that shuffled through the sawdust to the next spot at the bar, away from me. She never even looked at me, kept her eyes straight in front of her.

I moved into her old spot.

"Let's try this again," I said. "Your drink's still tequila? I've quit, you know."

"This person is not here," Michele said sternly.

"Who's not?" asked the bartender.

"Won't you even talk to me?" I asked.

Before she could answer, some guy in flannel shirt and jeans and black fishing boots up to his knees was practically in my face.

"There's a problem," he said, noticing his cigarettes were at the other end of the bar, yards from Michele.

"Peter," Michele said. "Tell this person that he isn't here."

"There's definitely a problem here," Peter said.

"The only problem here is that I'm not getting through," I said. "Come on, Michele. I came all this way. Let's get out of here and talk."

She said nothing.

"I don't think she talks to people that aren't here," Peter said.

"What kind of state is this?" I asked. "C'mon, five minutes, Michele."

"Son," the bartender told me, "this isn't a good idea. The lady has a lot of friends here...Maybe she'll talk tomorrow."

The guy's voice was low and calm, but it affected the bar in some way. Michele left her place, never once looking in my direction, and when I tried to follow her, that Peter guy got in my way and more than a few chairs scraped out from beneath their tables. Oh, great, I was thinking. I come all the way to Alaska and get the shit kicked out of me.

"This is ridiculous!" I shouted. I took the time to light a cigarette and looked into the eyes of as many of these "friends" I could.

"Son," the bartender started.

"Yeah, yeah," I said, flipping a buck onto the bar. "Thanks for nothing."

But I was gone for only a minute. I had two years of patience. One more day? Bullshit.

The boy paused and lit a cigarette. I lit another. We both proved the stereotypes about recovering alcoholics trading one addiction for another.

"Let me get this straight," I said. "You drove all the way to Alaska to propose to some girl you hadn't talked to in two years?"

"Crazy, like I said."

"I don't know," I said. "I guess. So what happened?"

"Well, before I charged back into the Salty Dawg, I took five one hundred dollar bills from my wallet and folded them into my pocket, right over the engagement ring."

"Wait I minute," I said. "You hoped to bribe her into marriage? Boy, I don't know about you."

"No, no," he said. "I'll get to that."

I shoved open the door to the bar. It took me only a moment to spot her near the back. She was at a small table with what's-his-face. Donny.

"I drove all the way from South Dakota to talk to that woman," I announced, pointing to Michele. "I'm not leaving till I do."

I began walking right through that crowd. As soon as Michele stood up and let out a little peep, the whole freaking bar, I swear, jumped me. But through the whole thing I was thinking, where'd these guys learn to bar fight? Hollywood? They might have started out together, but soon most of the punches being thrown were nowhere near me. I did get shoved to the ground, that's about it. Drinks flew, chairs splintered, people were saying "Fuck you" to anybody who'd listen. I think they were all just looking for an excuse to fight.

Sometime into it, I pulled free, took out the five bills, and flung them at Michele's feet.

"Take this, at least," I said quickly. "I owe you."

I didn't even see if she got the money. Somebody pulled me back into the fight by my shirt collar. Something icy cold, like a frozen margarita, splashed across my back. Half a lime bounced off my nose. Some woman with a rose tattoo on her shoulder took a whack at my ankle with the leg of a chair. Suddenly, these guys seemed to figure out who started it, for at once they all turned on me, each grabbing a handful, and rifled me past the damage and out the door. I felt like I'd been chewed up then spit out through a straw.

"Long way to go to get bounced out of a bar," I said, helping myself to another Coke out of the two-liter bottle.

"Tell me about it," he said. "Stupid thing is, all the changes I've made. Getting off booze. Working my way up to manager at Long John Silver's, the night classes, avoiding my old pals. I convinced myself that all of that was for us, for me and Michele. I didn't bother to check if any of it would matter to her."

"It wasn't all for you two," I said. "Don't think that. Don't start knocking sobriety. You don't need a reason to get sober."

He nodded and lit up another. "Story's not quite finished."

I sat back.

I climbed into my truck, pulled up near the door to the Salty Dawg and rolled down my window. The gravel and clamshell parking lot was packed with pick-ups and rusting hatchbacks. Inside, the jukebox was humming out Motown. Glasses tinkled, chairs scraped across the wooden floor, heavy boots pounded the planks. Above all this was laughter and shouting. So much for the fight. The whole town was buzzing in there, alive, dancing through the night like it had all the years before I ever showed my face.

I pulled back onto the road. Without even thinking about it, I was heading home. I'd given up, just like that. But then I remembered all the fishing gear I bought. Two hundred dollars, I spent. I read somewhere that August was the best time to catch salmon in Alaska. They'd be coming home to spawn. This was the only reason I needed to stick around Homer for a while.

The Salty Dawg is on Homer Spit. Both sides of the spit are lined with beaches. I pulled off the road a few hundred yards from the Salty Dawg and trudged down to the water's edge. It took me an hour to figure out how to cast that new rod. Two years ago I would've given up after ten minutes and thrown the damn thing into the ocean. But I fiddled with it and figured out the flip of the wrist it took to send the line far and straight into the murky water. My feet were planted inches from the water line. The salmon splashed just a few yards ahead. The inside of my nose was caked with sea salt. Mountains rose in front of me, the peaks so close to the water, so near Homer Spit, I felt I could broad jump across the water and land on one.

Past midnight it must have been when Michele popped back into my life. I heard her laugh and her "thank you" before anything else. A truck sped away. I looked toward the sky. That's where the sounds seemed to come from. But the sky was empty, too light for stars even. Alaska. Land of the Midnight Sun and all that. I reeled my line back in, afraid to look behind me. Then cast again into the growing darkness. A second later Michele was next to me, holding out two hundred and fifty dollars.

"The whole thing cost five hundred," she said. Her voice was light and airy again, like I remembered it, but I don't know, it sounded kind of forced.

"Don't think you were all responsible," she went on. "I know what birth control is, too."

"Keep it," I said, trying to look like I was wrapped up in my fishing. All I could think about was pulling her to the sand and kissing her. "You can't be making a lot of money at that place."

"I make enough," she said. She shoved the cash into my pocket, right back over the engagement ring. I shivered over the light pressure on my thigh." "Take it back," I said, "or I'll throw it into the ocean." I kept my eyes in front of me, like Michele had in the Salty Dawg, and turned the reel slowly. Childish, I know. I was thrilled she was there. My expectations mounted again. She could have mailed me the money.

"Nice friends you got," I said. "I haven't been thrown out of a bar in over two years."

"You bet they are," she said.

We didn't say anything for what seemed like an hour. What was I expecting, some kind of Hollywood reunion? Two lovers spend the whole movie treating each other like shit, then somewhere near the end they forgive one another, then they're hugging and kissing and walking on a beach?

"You found me," I said.

"Not too many trucks around with a South Dakota license plate," she said. "You're just crazy! Coming all this way."

The sing-song in her voice was back and sounding real. It was getting darker out on the bay. Nothing but murk. The horn of a far away boat sounded, but other than that the only thing to hear was the click of the line I kept slowly reeling in.

Michele plopped down into the sand and rolled a cigarette. When she was done I reached down and lit it.

"No filters?" I asked. Nothing else came to my mouth.

"I like rolling," Michele said. "It's fun. You should try it. Besides, I don't smoke as much this way."

"I'll stick to the old fashioned kind," I said, lighting up a Marlboro. I dropped my pole and sat down next to Michele. She was staring out to sea. When she pulled on her cigarette, the cherry lit up her cheeks, making them look sunken. I could really imagine her skull then.

"I was just thinking," I started. "I was just thinking about the time we were driving down to Texas to see your sister. Remember that? We showed *up late at the campsite on the Mississippi, in Iowa? It was so late and so dark. We couldn't see anything, except the moon reflecting off the river. And the river was so wide and was moving so fast."*

She'd been looking me over then, but soon as I stopped talking she moved her eyes back to the sea.

"Remember how we finally got to sleep," I continued. "Only at about four a train came. It was so damn loud, we thought we were about to be run down. When it was gone we looked out the tent and figured out we had pitched it about ten yards from the tracks."

I laughed softly, but it sounded too loud in the clear air. I wanted Michele to remember how we touched each other after the train rode by. Her eyes were so bright that night and so trusting. That train could have been inside of me my heart beat so fast. I'd bet my truck she fell in love with me that night, too.

"Right here, right now," I said, "I just thought of that night. This night reminded me. They seem the same."

But she didn't say anything. After a few minutes more of silence, she stretched and got up, went right to the other side of me and picked up the fishing pole.

"You have a worm on this," she said in her sing-song voice. "A plastic worm!"

Did she hear anything I said?

"I didn't have much luck with it," I said. "Maybe I should try a different color."

Michele shook her head and laughed. She fingered through my tackle box and found a mean looking hook with three long, sharp barbs. She replaced the worm with it.

"You do this often?" I asked.

"Sure," she said. "Try it."

I stood up and took the pole and sent the hook out into the night. I reeled it back in slowly, like I'd been doing all night.

"You'll never catch anything like that," she said.

"I never fished much," I said. "Not since I was a kid."

"Let me," she said. "This is snagging season." She took the pole and cast. The singing line seemed to fly for a full minute. It went way out there. Once she'd locked the line and reeled in the slack, she jerked the pole to her

left. She then swung the pole back in front of us, reeling quickly. She was serious. I felt sorry for anything that would swim into her path. She kept up with this jerk and reel combo until that mean hook was swinging above the water in front of us.

"Jesus," I said. "You never did that back home."

"You try," Michele said. "The way I did it."

With more strength before, I flipped the line out. As far as I could tell, it didn't go nearly as far as Michele's. I tried the reel and jerk just like Michele had, but something didn't feel right. Before I knew it, that hook was tangled at the top of the pole.

"Well," I said. "Guess the fish are further out."

"It's in the wrist," she said. "It don't take Arnold Schwarzenegger to get her out there. Try again."

"Why don't you try again?"

"It's your pole," she said. "And you can't come to Alaska without getting a fish. It's a rule. Everybody gets a fish."

I flipped the line back out. This time, it did go further, and the jerk and reel felt more natural.

"About a week after I got here there was a halibut derby," Michele said. "There is every year. I had never been out on a boat before. But some guys dragged me out and stuck a pole in my hands. Before you know it, I caught a huge one. Two hundred pounds!"

"No shit?"

"No shit," Michele said. "It took an hour to get her out of the water. Once we got her up she swayed and was swinging and crashing into things. I thought she was going to kill me. Then the captain stepped up with a rifle and shot two bullets into the poor thing's head."

"With a gun? Who'd shoot a fish with a gun."

"A smart guy. This was a big fish. Tasted good, too. So you have to get a fish."

I kept recasting.

"You're getting the hang of it," she said, rolling another cigarette.

I snagged almost an hour. My forearms and legs were getting really sore. But it was nice, just small talk about Alaska and South Dakota. We were comfortable, I think, and I began to wonder if my going up there wasn't so crazy after all.

"Listen," I said. "You know why I'm here, right?"

"I guess so."

"There's an engagement ring in my pocket. Underneath the money you stuffed down there."

I cast again and looked over to her. She'd gone stone faced.

"I'll tell you about the ring," I said. And as I went on with the story, me yanking back the pole seemed to end every sentence. "I bought that ring two years ago. It's the same one, I swear. The moment after we hung up, right after you told me you were pregnant, I went straight to my brother and told him what I had in mind. He loaned me some money. I went straight to the mall and picked the ring out. I was all for it, Michele. I was on my way to your place when, I don't know. Something snapped. I didn't stop. Next thing I knew I was sleeping one off in a jail in Iowa."

And that's the moment I caught the fish. Right in mid-confession.

"Shit!" I said.

"Keep that line taut," Michele said. "Don't give him any slack or he'll tear the pole out of your hands."

"Christ, he's a whale." I pulled the pole across my chest and tried to reel him in, but the line barely budged. I moved my left hand to the pole itself and somehow got the cork handle anchored in the crook of my right arm.

"That's it," Michele said. "Keep him coming."

"Jesus, I can barely..." My whole body was into pulling that thing from the water. I'd either get him out, or he'd dragged me in. Felt like my muscles were about to pop and the skin from my hands torn off.

"It's gonna snap," I yelled.

"Hold on," Michele said. "Don't give the sucker any slack!"

I got him in an inch at a time. After what must have been a half hour, there was a sudden splash and the King salmon's silver belly flashed under the moonlight. Michele jumped into the water with the net and scooped him out.

"I'd call him at twenty pounds," she said. "Good one!"

"It felt like two hundred," I said. Wiped out, I sat down and leaned back on my elbows.

"They're fighters," Michele said. She dropped the net with the fish between us. The hook was lodged in the salmon's side. Only a small drop of blood was coming out. Michele slipped the hook out and flung away the line. Saying nothing, we watched the fish die.

Sitting there, that fish looking up at me, it was impossible not to think about the kid Michele and me almost had. Had I stopped with the ring the first time we would've been in bed in Sioux Falls wondering if the kid would sleep, not in Homer, Alaska staring at a dying salmon.

Maybe the fish struck Michele in the same way, or maybe she could read my mind.

"I wouldn't have kept that baby no matter what," she said.

"I don't understand," I said.

She cupped her forehead in her hands. She was sitting with her long legs hitched up. She tried to say something, I know, but couldn't just then. Her lips kept moving but nothing came out. Instead, she pulled out a Swiss army knife and turned out the leather punch. With the other hand she grabbed the fish and stuck her thumb underneath his gill, into the back of his throat, then with the leather punch made a slit from the sperm hole to her thumb. She opened up the belly, made two quick cuts under the gills and scooped out the sac of guts.

"Jesus," I said.

She flung the guts into the ocean.

"It's a living," she said. "At work they call me the Slime-Line Queen. I'm the best!" She pushed down the leather punch and pulled out the longest blade. The tip had been filed round. She bent closer to my fish and made another cut along his spine, through the thick bloodline. With one swift flick she swept out the blood.

She looked at me. A trail of blood had hit her on the cheek, starting at the corner of her lips.

"Your fish," she said.

Now it was my turn to bury my head in my hands.

"Back some time ago, about six months before you left?" I said. "I lied when I said I didn't remember hitting you. I remembered it. I remember it every day of my life. I'm changed now. I'd never do it again."

"I believe you," she said.

"I thought about just taking the ring out of my pocket and holding it in my open hand," I said. "Then, if you didn't take it, right now, I'd toss it into the water."

I went ahead and took the ring out and rolled it between finger and thumb.

"I was shocked when you didn't show up that day," she said.

I started to apologize, but she plowed ahead, like I wasn't even there.

"But when I woke up the next morning and you still weren't there, I was the happiest I'd ever been. You were gone and I was going to have a beautiful baby. But by the afternoon I realized I couldn't keep the baby, because she wasn't my baby. She was our baby. And as long as she was part of my life, you would be too."

She took a deep breath and looked out to sea.

"You didn't want me around so you killed our baby?"

"Yes," she said sharply. "And that's the thing I remember every day of my life."

I sat on that a moment.

"Your sister didn't tell me what you did until after you left. Guess she'd thought I'd try to stop you," I said.

"She's my best friend."

"I've changed, you know," I said. "I stopped drinking when I heard what you'd done. Now I have a good job, too."

"I'm glad for you," she said.

"Well, I'll save us some trouble, for once." I flicked the ring into the ocean, to about where my fish had broken the surface, like I would a spent cigarette.

"I'm sorry," Michele said. She was still looking out to sea, to where the moonlight opened a path on the water.

"And that's how it ended," the boy said. "She apologizing to me. Isn't that crazy? I just picked up my fish and went back to my truck. As I pulled away, I looked out to the water. She still sat where I left her.

"And then I came home."

I lit a cigarette.

"Driving up there took some guts," I said. "I wouldn't have done it, drunk or sober."

He nodded.

"This is the fish, I take it?"

"Most of it's in the freezer."

"You ever want to share some more of it," I said, "don't hesitate to call."

"Was I crazy?" he asked.

I looked over to the television. The Vikes were pinned deep in their own territory, but it didn't matter because the game was almost over and they were down three touchdowns.

"No, you weren't crazy," I said. "After she had that abortion you bottomed out, right?"

"I don't remember much, but yeah."

"And then you got better. If you didn't bottom out, where'd you be now? Drunk and stupid. That's a hard truth. When you stop drinking it seems like you give up the world, but you have to give it up for something else. She gave up something, too, remember. Both of you did. Now you can move on."

He nodded again. We watched the last few minutes of the game in silence. I couldn't think of anything else to say. The truth, really, was too harsh. I knew what he was thinking. Back when, while he was on the bottle, at least he wasn't alone.

"There might be a movie on," he said. "If you want to stick around."

That sounded fine by me, since I had no one at home to answer to. I poured us both some more Coke and settled back into the couch.

A Man Loves His Cat

Peter didn't like animals. And even if he did, well, this was Alaska. He could walk out of the apartment building and encounter moose, eagles, bears, whatever. He didn't need a pet. But there was Sanda placing a moldy cardboard box on Peter's living room floor. She reached down and lifted out a kitten, a tiny kitten, mostly black and spattered with white spots, as if someone had squirted it with bleach.

"Isn't she adorable?" Sanda rubbed noses with the kitten, and then settled her back into the box.

"It's a cat," Peter said, brushing away the ivory dust that had fallen from box to nice, clean rug. He tilted the box. The kitten tried to climb up the side, but collapsed before it made it to the top.

"Meow!" the kitten squeaked, her bony head shuddering.

"Meow! Meow! Meow!" Sanda echoed. She took back the box and thrust her head into it.

"It's a cat," Peter repeated. "I'm not supposed to have pets in my apartment."

"But Smoky is just a kitten, such a small thing," Sanda said. Her voice was muffled, because her head was still in the box. Peter couldn't see her face, only the kitten's paws which were grabbing for her ears.

"Smoky?" Peter asked. "Boner" would be more appropriate, he thought.

"Meow! Meow!" Sanda said, removing her head from the box. "I hope you don't mind that I already named her."

"Smoky the cat," Peter said.

"Smoky can be our pet," Sanda said. "We'll both take care of her."

She dumped over the box. Smoky jumped out and sprinted across the room, leaping over invisible barriers before burying itself under Peter's favorite, and only, chair.

Peter walked over and slumped down into the cushions. He finished off his beer. It had gotten warm.

"It's a cat." He sighed.

"It's our cat," Sanda said. "Besides, it's only temporary. Once Ja-
nice and her mangy dog move out I'll keep Smoky at my place. You
can visit whenever you want."

Is that when I move in? Peter wanted to ask. But he knew better.
They had that discussion before. Sanda's canned answer was, "It's not
a good idea."

"It's not a good idea," Peter said.

Sanda frowned, then pouted, then stretched out onto her stomach.
She slithered toward Peter until her head was between his feet.

"Meow," she whispered, now on her side, her face pressed into the
rug. Peter felt her hand rummaging beneath his seat, heard the
kitten's claws bite into the legs.

Sanda stood. The carpet had left red indentations like worms on
one cheek. She grinned and lowered herself onto Peter's lap. They
kissed. When Peter went for her breasts, Sanda pushed his hands
away.

"Honey, not now," she said. "You know I have class."

"Later?"

"Later."

Thirty minutes after Sanda left for her class at Homer's one building community college, Peter stepped over the meowing kitten and
went to the kitchen for a beer. The kitten followed him.

Sanda hadn't brought cat food. Milk, Peter thought. Of course,
there was no milk. He hadn't had milk since he left his parent's trailer
a year and a half earlier. Now he subsisted on beer and Cheeto's, take
out pizzas and anything he managed to snag out of Kachemak Bay.
These days, he only got square meals when he was working at Seward
Fisheries and had access to their cafeteria. There hadn't been work
there for a couple weeks.

For his own dinner, Peter took out a mangled salmon steak to de-
frost. He opened a Coke and sloshed some into a bowl for the kitten.
Smoky slurped tentatively before backing away.

"Stupid cat." Peter kicked the bowl across the floor, splashing the
kitten with Coke. Instead of running away, Smoky walked over to
Peter and rubbed up against his legs.

"One stomp with my foot..." He bent down and held the kitten's jaw. He remembered Sanda's promise of "later." Maybe she'd spend the night.

"Boner," he said. "What exactly are you doing here?" He reached around the head to pick her up, to hold him to his chest, but she sprang away from his grasp.

***

The next morning, Peter, bleary-eyed and groggy, stepped into a steamy pile of feces. In the kitchen, Smoky was sitting tall and proud next to a chewed sock. She scampered over to Peter and purred. He regretted buying the over-priced cat food from the bait shop the night before.

"Do I pay for it on every end?" He kicked the kitten away. He picked up the phone and punched out Sanda's number.

"Hello?"

"Sanda. I thought you were coming over last night."

"My period started. You know how I am. How's our baby?"

"It shit..."

"It is a she," Sanda said.

"She shit on my rug. My rug. And I stepped in it. How am I going to get rid of the smell?"

"It's not worth getting angry over," Sanda said. "We'll train her."

"Could you come over now?"

"We'll see."

"Dammit!" Peter dropped the phone. Smoky was squatting into a position that could mean only one thing. Peter grabbed her by the scruff of the neck and looked around wildly as the kitten dribbled urine onto his bare legs.

"Bathroom! Bathroom!" he yelled, running down the hall. In the bathroom he flipped up the toilet lid and held the kitten over the bowl. She meowed. Peter threw her into the shower stall and slammed the door.

The line was dead when he got back to the phone.

***

Peter had just stuffed a box of three hundred envelops for Mutual Life Insurance when Sanda knocked on the door. She held a ten-pound bag of kitty litter and got angry when Peter told her where Smoky was.

"She pissed on me and crapped on the floor," he explained.

"Well, what do you expect? She's just a baby." Sanda retrieved the kitten from the bathroom.

"Little love, kissy kiss." She kissed Smoky on the mouth.

"She chewed up my sock," Peter said.

"You can't lock her up," Sanda said. "She'll turn into a psycho. Right, kitty? Little sweetness."

In the kitchen, Sanda dumped some litter into an empty Coke carton.

"I don't know how to train a cat," Peter said.

Smoky sniffed the box.

"It's easy," Sanda said.

"Forget it," Peter said. "If you don't take her to your place I'll chuck her into the bay."

"Don't say that!" Sanda said. "We'll train her. We can do it." She unbuckled Peter's belt.

"What about your period?"

"False alarm."

***

For the first time in three weeks Peter awoke next to Sanda. He watched her sleep, saw little bubbles form at the corners of her open mouth, listened to her snore. He kissed her awake. Twenty minutes later, when she opened the bathroom door to leave for her 8:30 "Fantastic Literature" class, wearing the T-shirt he had received for placing ninth in last year's Halibut Derby, Peter felt the creaky lid to his heart open wider.

This is love, he thought.

That day, Peter intended to plow through the rest of the envelops due to Mutual Life, but training the kitten took more time than he imagined; he had to watch her constantly, and after a few hours he discovered that Smoky had been urinating under his chair. Peter dumped an entire box of baking soda on the staining, wet carpet.

Forty minutes after Sanda was supposed to be back, she called.

"It's almost nine," Peter said.

"I know, but I got a surprise assignment."

"What about tomorrow?"

"You know tomorrow is Friday. I have to go to the observatory for Astronomy Lab. How's our baby?"

"She pissed under my chair."

"I'll try to make it over for lunch tomorrow. Can you fix something?"

"Anything you want, babe. Last night was wonderful."

There was a pause.

"Something wrong?" Peter asked.

"I was purring," Sanda said.

The next morning Peter hitched to the tip of Homer Spit for fresh crab, sourdough rolls and a bottle of wine. When Sanda arrived at two, one hour after Peter expected her, the cod sandwiches were cold. Smoky had invaded the picnic on the living room floor and was lapping up chowder and nibbling crab salad.

"How cute!" Sanda said.

"The salad's okay cold," Peter said.

"I just came to see Smoky. Little darling! Come to mamma." She picked up the kitten and kissed her.

"Have you been using your litter box, cutie?" Sanda asked.

"Not once," Peter said. "It takes two people, I think."

"Bad little kitty," Sanda kissed her again. "I've got to get back to the library."

"But I thought we could go skating today," Peter said. "Beluga Lake is frozen enough."

"I'd love to, hon, but this damn assignment. Besides, someone's got to take care of the baby."

***

A week passed. Smoky continued to poop and pee under Peter's chair. Sanda made and broke dates. On the phone, she reminded Peter to buy food, and to change Smoky's water daily. A little fresh cream, she said, makes a great treat.

By Friday, Peter had had enough.

He decided to starve the kitten to death.

He felt powerful when Sanda called and he lied to her.

"I found some poop in the box," he said. "In fact, I'll probably change the litter tomorrow."

"How wonderful," Sanda said. "Our baby's growing up."

Peter looked down on the pathetic, dying creature. He imagined her weight quickly diminishing, her skin and hair dissolving, her muscle and sinew melting. A skeleton is all that would remain. Not a spotted black coat of fur, but an animation of fragile bones, like a prehistoric rat suddenly coming alive in museum, its ribs clacking together like marbles in a bag.

Before Peter went to bed that night, he tossed Smoky back into the shower stall. No food, no water. She meowed all night. Peter gave up on sleep at six. On his living room floor he lay out an arc of envelopes and advertisements for a shipment to Mutual Life. Cod was starting to come in at Sew-Fish. He had to report back to work on Monday. The envelopes had to be done.

But the meowing would not stop. Peter put on an Aerosmith record and turned it way up, but the meowing butted its way between songs, even seemed to be accompanying Steve Tyler. At times, Peter thought the kitten was finally winding down; her meows grew weaker and further apart. Then suddenly, the meows reached a new, impossibly high crescendo, as if for the first time Smoky had discovered a new way to talk.

Peter drank beer, jammed cotton into his ears, smoked some pot. Still, he couldn't work, couldn't even stuff some envelopes. The kitten wouldn't shut up. It was like a Poe story he had read some of in high school. He couldn't take it any longer. Starvation was too slow. Peter pushed aside the papers. He lifted up an end table and pulled away the "Complete Works of Shakespeare" which had been serving as a leg ever since Sanda gave it to him for his birthday. The table, one support gone, toppled to the floor, taking the second hand lamp with it. Peter, his heart pounding, marched into the bathroom, Shakespeare raised. When he opened the shower door, Smoky leaped. Not passed him, in hope of finding an open window, a means of escape from her tormentor but, with claws outstretched, onto Peter's pant leg.

"Jesus Christ!" Peter shook his leg, but Smoky clung to his jeans like a velcroed ball. Peter hopped about on one leg and tried to pry her off with the edge of the sink. That didn't work. He tossed the book into the shower and bent to rip off the kitten. She jumped and climbed Peter's body as if it was a telephone pole, yet somehow her claws only caught his clothes. He relaxed when she reached his beating heart. The kitten then slipped up to his shoulder and stuffed her wet nose into his ear.

Peter was defeated.

The following week, he slept well. Smoky curled into a ball beneath his comforter. Peter brought home pieces of fresh cod from work and blew his money on rubber toys and catnip. At one time, the empty evenings at home drove him to the bars that didn't care about drinking ages. Now he spent them with Smoky, or Boner, and laughed with delight when she attacked any strand of string he held in front of her, or when she chased a plastic squirrel around the apartment. After she pooped in her box for the first time, he set her on his shoulder and fed her pieces of fish from his own lips.

In the middle of the week, Peter finally heard from Sanda.

"She's completely trained," he told her. "And she likes to climb up to my shoulder."

"It's not fair!"

"What can I say," Peter said.

"What about Friday? That old Don Johnson movie's playing at midnight. Then we can go back to your place and play with Smoky."

"Midnight?"

"I've got Astronomy Lab," she pleaded.

***

Midnight approached. Sanda was twenty minutes late. She's stuck at the observatory, he thought. Maybe something extra special is going on up there; a comet, a supernova.

He put on a heavy sweater and jean jacket, and after giving Boner a kiss, stepped out onto the exposed walkway lining the second floor of his apartment building. He searched the sky, hoping to share something special with Sanda by gazing into the same star-filled bowl. All he saw, however, was cloud. Not one star, not even the moon.

"Fuck it," Peter said. He went back into his apartment. Boner's eyes glowed green in the dark. Peter traded the jean jacket for a loose fitting army coat. He swept up the kitten and dropped her into the largest pocket.

***

"Don Johnson?" he asked the cashier at the theater. Boner was purring in his pocket.

A pretty redhead with a black eye handed him a ticket for "A Boy and His Dog." Inside Homer's only theater, a layer of smoke hugged the ceiling and distorted the topmost section of the screen. Peter sat down next to a couple smoking hash out of a porcelain bong in the shape of a wizard. All shapes and sizes of pipes and bottles were passed around. Burning cherries lit up the theater like red giant stars in the dead of winter's night sky.

Peter took out the kitten and placed her on his shoulder. She purred, and sometimes raised a paw to catch a flying object on the screen. The movie was about a boy who lived in a post-holocaust earth. His only companion was a telepathic dog who had the ability to sniff out women for his virile master. Don Johnson played the boy, and eventually he fell for a girl who lived in an underworld city called "New Topeka." Don Johnson abandoned his dog to live in the underworld.

Before the movie ended, a hand clamped down on Peter's shoulder. He turned into the blazing beam of a flashlight.

"Hey, you can't bring that in here," shouted a voice from behind the light. "A cat, for Chrissake!"

So as Don Johnson sat in a machine that sucked out his sperm for the women of New Topeka, Peter walked toward the exit, kicking away empty beer bottles and saying "no" to the offerings of pot.

The next morning a loud knock woke up Peter. He left Boner snoozing in the jumble of blankets. Sanda was at the door, dressed smartly, Peter thought, in a long, wool skirt, a dress jacket with padded shoulders, sunglasses.

"You go to church or something?" Peter asked.

"Listen, Peter. We have to talk."

"Okay. You want a Coke?"

"It's about us."

"You better come in then," Peter said, opening the door wide. "Sit down." He hurried to the bedroom and pulled the door shut.

"I'm not staying," Sanda said. "Where's Smoky?"

"Boner's sleeping," Peter said. "We had a late night."

"Listen, Peter. We've had some great times together. But my life is changing. I'll have my degree soon."

"Uh-uh."

"I thought we'd make it, you know?" Sanda said.

"Uh-uh."

"You're a nice guy, and everything, but look at this place."

"Yeah."

"I have to think about my future."

"Okay."

"I loved you once, but frankly, you don't know what love is. It's a two-way street."

"I see."

"Where's Smoky?"

"Boner? Why do you ask?"

"Because I'm taking her. She's mine. Besides, you don't want her."

"Like you said, your life is changing. So's mine."

"It's too late for that," Sanda said.

"I'm keeping her," Peter said.

Sanda sprinted for the bedroom, but Peter was right on her tail.

"Smoky," Sanda called.

She opened the door. Peter yanked it shut.

69

"You're not taking her," he said.

"You're being childish," Sanda said. "You can't take care of her. And she's not happy here."

Peter kept a firm grip on the doorknob.

"Listen, be reasonable," Sanda said. "The woman always gets custody." She grabbed Peter's hand and tried to pull it off the doorknob.

"Go to hell." Peter pushed Sanda into the opposite wall.

"How dare you!"

Peter took hold of her arms and pushed her back into the living room.

"You son-of-a-bitch. I'll scream. Let go of me. She's mine, I tell you."

"Go to hell," Peter repeated.

"I swear, I'll sue," she screamed as he forced her out the door.

He slammed the door behind her, paced around his living room, his fists clenching and unclenching. Sanda hit the door with something, probably her foot. Peter picked up the Shakespeare and whipped it.

"Go to hell!" he yelled.

Eventually, he heard her creak along the walkway and down the stairs. He sat in his chair and stared absently at the dent the book had made in his door. Boner meowed. Peter ran into the bedroom and scooped her up.

"I don't know what love is," he muttered, smoothing back the kitten's ears. "Sure I know what love is. A man loves his cat."

To War

Three months after her husband went off to war, Annie sat at the table and watched the spaceships hover above the sparkling and pristine snow covering her backyard. Giant mushrooms, they seemed, their caps glowing green with some cosmic moss, and humming with a burning energy that beckoned Annie to the confines of their round shadows, majestic umbrellas. As inviting and dangerous as the foliage of a tall tree during a spring thunderstorm.

The phone rang. Before the first ring had ended, the mushroom caps were sucked up into the sky, back to their home base; to the moon, to Mars, to the stars, back to from wherever they had come.

Patricia was on the phone.

"He's going to die in a helicopter crash," she said.

Last week, while she and Annie watched the build-up to the war on television, Patricia's husband was going to die from Friendly Fire. The news showed a shot through a pilot's sight, how, when the little white circle was directly above a chimney, the pilot pushed a button and a missile spiraled into the tiny dark hole.

"He always sleeps on his back, mouth open. A pilot will make a mistake and bomb his barracks. The little missile will go down the chimney, into his mouth, and blow him to bits," Patricia had said.

"A helicopter, you say?" Annie asked, shifting the phone to her other shoulder.

"Some alcoholic pilot will go nuts from the shakes," Patricia said. "Over there, they can't even have light beer. The pilot will pass out, and the helicopter will go down, taking him with it. Can I come over?"

"Why not?" Annie replied, and hung up. Patricia was over nearly every day. She didn't have to ask.

Annie and Patricia became friends by accident. Two summers before, they worked together at a restaurant in Denali National Park. One week, both happened to have days off simultaneously. They were on the same Anchorage bound train, and not too far from the shopping malls and bars of Alaska's largest city, when a half ton of rock and dirt spilled from a slope hugging the line and slammed into the engine, burying a section of track. They were stranded only a mile north of Fort Richardson. A detachment of reserves was sent in to dig out the train.

Looking out at the tundra, Annie had felt something drop down into her stomach as the column of troops emerged from the low and scattered underbrush, picks and shovels slung over their shoulders like rifles. They attacked the rocks and the clumps of dirt striped with permafrost without orders, as if by instinct they were clawing for the confines of a foxhole. The passengers in the train watched quietly. Some had commandeered Chinook Ales from the dining car, others, most of them young women, never left their seats. They were content staring at the men who moved in fluid motions, how they swiped at the clouds of mosquitoes nipping at their necks while never losing their unified digging rhythm.

The marriages came within the following year. Patricia liked to think that she and Annie had fallen in love at the exact same moment. Annie wouldn't argue, but looking back, she knew she was struck first not by love, but by curiosity. She had been mesmerized by the machi-nations of the unit of men, the way the shirts on their backs gradually darkened with sweat and clung to working muscles. All the men were crowded in such a small area, she thought, yet the shining blades of the shovels and dangerous points of the picks were able, somehow, to find the creases between fragile flesh, falling with sharp edges through invisible grooves in an unchecked motion that was at once beautiful and disquieting.

There was a knock on the door. Patricia lived just one cabin over. When her husband went to war, she moved from the base and rented in Homer to be near Annie.

Patricia didn't wait for Annie to answer the door. She pushed it open and threw her coat, hat and gloves on the floor.

"Can we drink?" she asked. A flutter of snowflakes drifted in. She had a bottle in one hand, a pile of pictures in the other. She dropped the pictures on the table and took two glasses from the cupboard.

Annie looked. Patricia had taken a whole roll of herself nude.

"I'm going to send those to him," Patricia said. "I don't care what the Towel-heads say."

Most of the pictures were blurry. Patricia had posed herself on her feather bed. Some of the shots were of pouty lips, but taken too close to recognize as being Patricia's. In others, her legs were spread wide, or she had her butt pointed high towards the camera, or she was pushing her small breasts together to find some cleavage. In nearly every pose, a limb or two was cut off by the edge of the shot. Annie cupped these in her hand, and where the picture ended, wiggled her little finger to fill in a missing leg or arm.

Patricia filled the glasses with Crème de Menthe. The liquor looked like lime Kool-Aid. Both women stared at the glasses awhile, without reaching for them. They had talked about drinking before, how they were being dragged into a stereotype: the aging, potential war widow pining away for her husband, "General Hospital" or "All My Children" flapping by on the television, all the time slipping towards alcoholism and an addiction to valium, cemented to a chair, the cushions pieced around her soft, bulging butt. Rosy the Riveter was nostalgia. When the boats were in, which wasn't often in the dead of winter, Patricia and Annie slimed cod down at Sew-Fish. There were no planes to build, or scrap metal to collect. Today's war wife showed her support by wearing cheap ribbons and a T-shirt sporting a computer guided missile aimed for the Enemy's ass-hole.

"I'd rather get stoned," Patricia said.

"I don't have any," Annie said. She picked up her glass and drank the cool, syrupy liquor.

"Albie Monroe has some growing in his greenhouse," Patricia said.

Albie lived on the outskirts of Homer. Occasionally, Annie walked by his greenhouse on her way to an observation bunker left over from World War II. The little concrete hut had been stripped of its gun, and was now surrounded by barbed wire, not to protect it from Japanese soldiers who might tip-toe their way up the Aleutian chain, but from boys looking for a haven to drink beer and feel up their girlfriends. The barbed wire didn't stop anybody. But supposedly, some kind of chemical had leaked into the slope, the kind that could eat through the Wellington boots Patricia and Annie wore at Sew-Fish and turn skin phosphorescent orange. The threat scared most away, but that just made it a more meditative, peaceful place for Annie.

"Albie's got a gun," Annie said. She didn't want to share her special place with Patricia.

"Gun, schmun." Patricia drained her glass in one swallow. "This stuff turns my poop green."

"Did you see anything peculiar this morning?" Annie asked.

"Like what?"

"I don't know. In the sky. Weird lights."

"Northern lights?"

"No," Annie said. "Never mind. Maybe we should have some vodka."

"Vodka!" Patricia whined.

"Don't be a baby. I'll throw up before I get drunk on that," Annie explained, gesturing to the bottle.

"I can out drink you," Patricia said. "You're the baby."

For Christmas, Annie had received a bottle of Finnish vodka that had been infused with huckleberry. The cupboard underneath her sink was crammed with similar gifts. Even though she was only twenty, and never much of a drinker, family and friends saw she needed fortification against a winter made colder by her new husband's absence. Patricia had gotten the bottle of Crème de Menthe from her own well-stocked cupboard.

Annie poured two glasses of the purplish vodka and brought out the supplies the two women used to make paper snowflakes. They planned on filling a large box marked "Alaska Winter" and shipping it to their husbands. Patricia sipped her drink and absently took up scissors and paper. Neither woman talked much. They drank slowly and deliberately, and likewise, cut through the white construction paper as if they were using elaborate blueprints to make the snowflakes. When they took their time, more minutes seemed to pass.

By noon, the vodka had begun to work on Annie. The mail was late. The snowflakes, the alcohol, even the daily visits from Patricia were just means of passing time until the mail came. She leaned back in her chair. Her father had been a mailman, delivering to houses and businesses up and down the Kenai Peninsula, from Soldotna, back to Homer, and across the bay to Seldovia. On weekends, he woke Annie in the middle of the night, spilling his alcoholic breath on her face, to tell her about his time in Korea, how he blew Chink brains all over the trees and snow. Later, when Japanese investors began coming to Homer to scout out the fisheries, her father would form his hand into a gun, point at the person's head and yell "Bang!" Anyone Oriental would do.

Annie thought of him now, as she always did at about this time. She listened intently for the bit of "A Star Spangled Banner" the mail jeep's horn bleated out to announce the mail's arrival at the head of each street. She thought it funny that the mail "man," who had replaced her father, was a female Japanese immigrant who staged Homer's largest fireworks display in her backyard every Fourth of July.

Patricia was spending an inordinate amount of time on one flake. Her eyes were crossed and she was working a very detailed edge. Annie reached across and snipped it in half with her scissors.

"You bitch!" Patricia said.

Annie finished off the two fingers of vodka in her glass.

"I'm drunk," she said. "Let's get out of here."

Patricia threw her scissors onto the table and sat back with her arms crossed.

"That's stupid," she said. "She isn't here yet and there's all that snow in your driveway. Haven't you heard of a snow shovel?"

Annie already had on her coat and one boot.

"Annie, it's so wet out there. Why can't we just wait for the music like normal people?"

"Because." Annie had on both boots now. She whipped a scarf around her neck, jammed her fists into a brand new pair of mittens. She was out the door before Patricia got out of her chair.

The snow had let up, and the sun, which was hanging low in the sky, was beginning to break up the clouds. For the first time in weeks the mountain peaks across Kachemak Bay were popping into visibility. Annie kicked through the fresh, wet snow in her driveway. Her pick-up was almost completely buried and she wondered vaguely about the last time she had started it. Instead of giving that a second thought, she rushed behind the bed and formed a large snowball.

When Patricia entered the doorway, Annie heaved it. The snowball kissed off of Patricia's shoulder and flew into the cabin. Glass broke.

"Annie! You're wasted." Patricia shut the door behind her. "Yeah, I remember my first beer." She buttoned her coat to the very top and pulled her knit cap down. Very little of her face remained visible.

Annie was forming another snowball when she heard a distant tinkle. She dropped the snowball and jumped out into the plowed street. Patricia ran up behind her and took her arm. Both women blanketed their expectancy and nervousness with giggles as they made their way up the street to the mail boxes. The tinkle became louder, turning into notes of the national anthem. As the mail jeep began to slide to a stop, the women turned away and pretended not to notice. They still giggled, but their arms were tight in each other's grasp. When the jeep pulled away, they ran, slipping and sliding, to the mailboxes.

Annie suspected that Lin, the mail "man," would have paused and announced a letter from overseas. She knew Patricia and Annie; Homer was a small town. Still, Annie crossed her fingers. The only piece she received today, however, was her husband's Visa bill. It looked awfully small in the dark mailbox. She took it out and let it slip through her fingers. For the moment, she felt sober.

Patricia was sniffling. All she got was the newest "Ms." magazine. She leafed through it and hid her wet cheeks behind the flipping pages.

"Wynona Ryder looks stupid with blond hair," she said.

Annie tore the magazine from Patricia's hands and skipped back to her cabin.

"Annie! You're such a bitch today."

Instead of heading for the door, Annie trampled through the virgin snow of her front yard. When she got around the corner of the cabin she tossed aside the magazine and made two quick snowballs. She peered around the corner. As soon as Patricia hit the foot of the driveway, Annie whipped the two snowballs. The first one sailed high but the second hit Patricia square in the stomach. She doubled over, more likely out of surprise than pain–her coat was very thick–then ducked behind the pick-up truck.

Annie circled around the cabin to the top of the driveway. Patricia was scrabbling in the snow. Surely the crunching of her boots would give Annie away, but she only needed a couple of seconds. As soon as she reached the front of the truck, she sprinted through the knee-high snow as best she could and found Patricia, still hunched over, making snowballs. Before her friend could turn around, Annie slammed a snowball onto the back of her head. Patricia slumped forward and Annie ran off again, this time to the group of pines separating the friends' cabins.

Patricia must have been really mad, Annie thought, because she didn't even scream or whine, just jumped up and pulled away the back of her coat to let out the snow and ice. Then she scooped up a pile of snowballs and began marching towards the stand of pines.

"You fucking bitch," Patricia said. "You're dead."

They had done this before, back in October on the day before the boys left. Patricia had played fast-pitch softball all through school. Annie was accurate, but threw with too much loft, just like a girl. She was no match without her husband. Trickery and surprise had worked up until this point, but she needed something else. She dropped a snowball to the ground and began rolling it through the trees.

Patricia missed with her first shot. Annie just kept rolling her snowball. It quickly turned into a boulder.

"This should be good," Annie said.

Patricia was still breathing hard, but she never stayed mad for very long.

"Good for what?" she asked.

"Why don't you take one of those balls melting in your hand and start rolling," Annie said. "It'll take forever if I have to do all the work."

"Annie," Patricia complained.

Annie tossed away her sweat-soaked scarf and started another boulder.

"All right, already," Patricia said. She made her own boulder and rolled it next to the first two.

"I don't believe this," Patricia said. "How are we going to lift them on top of each other? We had the boys last time."

"We'll manage."

All winter long, the wind had been lifting off the rough waters of Kachemak Bay, snaking around the squat buildings and small woods of Homer, before arriving with force on Glacier View, Annie's road. What wind hadn't crept past her windowpanes and under her front door had blown a bowl into the snowfall between the pines and her cabin. The snow was not very deep in the center, and where the women's paths met, patches of grass poked through so that the yard began to look like a large checkerboard.

After a half hour they had a lower wall and three loose boulders, one of which had picked up some moose droppings. Squatting on opposite sides, the women embraced the boulders, locked hands, and lifted them on to the top of the lower wall. They filled in the joints with loose snow, and continued their work until the boulders formed a half-circle three layers high. Then they both sunk to their knees and admired the snow fort.

"The best this town's seen," Annie said.

"Never seen better," Patricia said.

"Who gets it?" Annie asked.

"Who gets what?"

"The fort. Who gets the fort?"

"Annie!"

"Well, you don't think I built it just to look at it," Annie said. "You can have it now, then we'll switch."

"I'm trashed, Annie."

Annie flung snow into Patricia's face, and then darted to the side of her cabin. She kicked over the empty garbage cans. One lid would make a shield. She piled the other with snowballs. Her shield raised, she crawled to the corner of the cabin. A snowball exploded on the side wall, spraying her with shrapnel.

"The enemy has been engaged," Annie said, swiping away the remnants of snow. She hunkered back to safety to consider her options. If she kept low behind her shield, she would be able to creep up on the fort. A problem, however, was that one hand held the shield, the other dragged the ammo. She had to stop to throw. But if she moved quickly enough and resisted firing before she got into effective range, she just might again catch the enemy unawares. Then, pounce and strike!

Annie eased away from the protection of the cabin. She remained low to the ground and held her shield far in front of her in order to limit the target area of her body. She began counting, intending to begin a mad scramble to the fort on a count of "three."

On "two," Patricia unleashed. One after another, four snowballs pounded into the shield, sending a shockwave through Annie's arm up into her skull. The last hit threw her onto her back and sent her, on all fours, to the confines of the cabin.

"You're dead," Patricia yelled. "Give up!"

Annie had left one of the garbage can covers in the middle of the yard. That arm of Patricia's, she thought, breathing heavily. I don't stand a chance.

"Never!" Annie yelled back.

Annie could wait it out. Eventually Patricia would tire of crouching in the snow and would come out for lunch or another drink. A castle siege, just like in the old days. As soon as Patricia left the fort, Annie would get her shot.

A quick reconnaissance to see what's what, then Annie could settle back against the warmth of her cabin. Still on her knees, she crawled to the corner. Her clothes itched her hot skin. She raised her palm in a salute to cut the glare of the sun and took a peek.

Patricia was anticipating. As soon as Annie caught sight of the fort, her view filled with white, and then there was an angry punch to her nose and eyes and astonished mouth. Again, she was thrown back. She got up choking on ice. She spit it up and it came out salty and red. She touched her nose and upper lip and felt her blood flow. Her head suddenly ached, and for the first time, she really felt the cold wetness that had soaked into her jeans.

"Annie?" Patricia called out tentatively.

Annie tried to answer but nothing came out. She got to her feet wobbling and nudged aside her shield and her little pile of snowballs. Blood dripped from her chin onto the snow. She looked full into the sun until her eyes burned and watered even more. Something clicked inside of her, and before it registered in her mind, her feet, her legs, her whole body was moving at full speed around the corner of her cabin and heading straight toward the fort. Patricia's head popped up and her eyes grew wide. Someone screamed. Annie leaped and flew, careening off the top of the fort, taking off an inch of ice that fanned out like buckshot. Patricia was already leaning back when the full weight of Annie struck her. The women, one pile soaked with sweat and snow, hit the tamped ground like a felled tree.

They lay there. Even through the layers of clothes, Annie could feel Patricia's heartbeat. It was so loud and insistent that Annie couldn't distinguish it from her own. She raised her bleeding face. Patricia took a long look, and then pulled it back down, back into the confines of her scarf. She murmured something unintelligible and held onto her friend's head. Annie cupped Patricia's shoulders and dug her fingernails through her mittens into her friend's coat. Both women were silent then, both clutched desperately for what was real.

The First Snow of Spring

During the night, as the weatherman promised, the jet stream swirled back into Alaska and squatted right on top the Kenai Peninsula and Prince William Sound, pushing aside the most recent warm spell. Donald looked out the window and up to the sky where the sun was trying to push its feeble way through the dense cloud cover. He dreaded his day of work. He was hung over, and neither orange juice nor coffee could wash away from the back of his throat the bitter aftermath of a night of Captain Morgan's spiced rum and the home-grown dope he had stolen out of his neighbor's greenhouse. He jammed his pockets with packages of M&Ms and Skittles. When he stepped out of his one-room cabin the wind hit his already aching head like a fist. On his way to school, where his bus waited, he gulped down a stale Pop Tart and chased it with M&Ms. He prayed that the change in weather hadn't made his charges antsy.

April had brought longer days, more time for the lingering Northern sun to melt down winter. The permafrost, however, kept the ground as hard and resistant as a marble slab; the snow that melted during the warm spell had remained on the surface in pools and wide rivulets, which were now again frozen. The streets were slick. The mud the melt had upended formed ugly, grey streaks that were trapped in the snow banks lining the sides of the roads. The heavy weight of the bus, and the chains enrobing its thick wheels helped, but from the moment of his first pick-up near the airport, to his delivery at the school on the fringe of Homer proper, Donald needed all his concentration to keep the bus from sliding off the bridge spanning Beluga Lake, or slamming into stalled pick-ups. As he struggled with the steering wheel, he cursed his buddies, the ones with balls at least, who were probably at that very moment chasing tail at the university in Anchorage. The only saving grace this morning was the kids were subdued.

After school, however, the kids turned. They tossed each other's notebooks out the windows, and threatened to push open the back emergency door and jump out while the bus sped down Homer bypass. They splattered spit balls against the front windshield and, with rubber bands, fired paper clips into the back of Donald's neck.

Donald was still on the fringe of his hangover, and tried to keep a clear head, thinking as he pulled the bus over to its first stop, that not too long ago he was one of them back there, flying paper airplanes into fresh new hairdos, fingering obscene pictures into the layer of frost covering the windows, maneuvering for the back seats. The kids, he knew, were impatient for summer. Just yesterday it seemed as if the warm sun was about to come out for good. Soon they'd be fishing the streams for Silver salmon until midnight, their parents working hard and late at the fish processing plants and on the docks of Homer Spit; at the restaurants and motels to accommodate the quick influx of tourists from Anchorage and the Lower Forty-Eight; at the many saloons, the grocery stores, the gas stations, the campgrounds. All to make up for the absence of work, the lack of money in an Alaskan winter. But the kids were ready to pick wild blueberries, to hunt for clams on the beach, to find their first kiss in the thick undergrowth of the woods behind Homer, the grasses and wild flowers still pungent with the smell of a wandering grizzly.

He pulled the bus over, and his first drop-offs made their way down the aisle. Donald forced a smile, and said, "Take care," to the last kid out. The boy turned and sneered at him, even refused Donald's offering of Skittles.

"Brat," Donald said, loud enough for only the boy to hear. As soon as Donald pulled away from the curb, the first drop-offs started bombarding the bus with snowballs. Before they departed the bus, they had opened most of the windows on one side. An old trick Donald remembered well. Behind him, snow and ice exploded like cannon shot. He watched in the mirror as the kids dove in desperation behind their seats, holding note-books above their heads to shield themselves, but laughing the whole time. Donald was chuckling to himself as well, when a perfectly aimed snowball spiraled through a window and smacked him behind his right ear. White shrapnel sprayed the driver-side window; the bulk of the projectile dropped behind him, into his seat. One boy in the back jumped up and started cheering, raising his hands to someone outside. Donald shook away the pain and slammed on the accelerator. The boy bounced off the back door and landed on his hands in the center aisle that had been mucked up with tramping boots and dirty ice. Kids who had been "pogoing"–kneeling down, boots flat on the layer of snow on the street, hanging onto the bumper with their hands for a free carnival ride–fell sprawling to their backs, the bus coughing out a black cloud of exhaust over them.

"Now, settle down!" Donald yelled. He wiped snow and water from his hair, and turned the bus onto Pioneer Avenue, the main thoroughfare of downtown Homer. The kids became quiet. Many of their parents worked on this road, or hung out in front of the employment agency.

Part of Donald wanted to laugh along with the kids, but damn it, he was the authority figure on the bus; he had to separate himself from his passengers. With the impact of the snowball still ringing in his head, he recalled how, when he was eight, he first went to work on his father's fishing boat. It was the same year his mother gave up on his father, and on Alaska, and went away to New York City. Every year until his father's accident, Donald spent the warm summer days on board, first repairing the nets and scrubbing the decks, and then as he grew stronger, helping to haul in the catch and shovel it into the hold. As he grew wiser to the temperament of the sea, he stood alongside his father, with his mind on the nautical charts and maps of the fishing grounds, and his eyes on the deceptive skies above Cook Inlet. Every year they struggled, barely breaking even after they paid the rest of the crew. Many other fishermen became rich, spending winters in Hawaii with their kids, some of which Donald now ferried around on this bus.

The very boat that Donald had fished on for ten years now sat in dry dock. After his father's death, the bank had foreclosed on the house. But Donald, with a little help from the man who had sold it to his father, managed to hold onto the boat. Fear kept him off the water. Every time he thought of taking up fishing once again, the image of his father's body washing up on the beach blackened by the Spill in Prince William Sound scared him into indecisiveness. He couldn't fish, anymore than he could unload the boat for college expenses.

The next stop was on Bartlett Avenue, just past the health food store. The road was on a steep incline. Now that they were off Pioneer, the kids started to rumble again. Donald meant not to let anyone else off the bus until all the windows were closed, but the kids' submissiveness on Pioneer lulled him into forgetting. He didn't remember until the kids were off the bus, and he had pulled back into the center of the road. Just then, like a prelude to an approaching storm, a gust of wind tore through the open windows; right on its tail another round of snow and ice came bursting into the bus. The kids remaining on board erupted again. Donald cursed, but the kids screamed too loudly to hear, and started chucking the pancakes of snow and ice sticking to seats and windows. The bus was rocked by the wind outside, and the now uncontrollable children inside, and all Donald could think to do was again slam on the accelerator, anything to get away from the bombardment, but the back wheels spun in place. Not able to move forward, the bus swerved to its side, and finally, when the tires found something to grab onto, the bus jolted and did a tailspin. The kids then screamed in real terror, their bodies thrown to one side, books and pencils flying out of their hands, and Donald, desperately trying to pull on the wheel, not knowing where or how to steer, bit clean into his lip before the bus was turned around completely and started sliding sideways down the hill. Finally, one back wheel bit into a patch of cement at the intersection of Pioneer and the bus jerked to a stop.

The descent of the bus quelled the kids into silence. The first drops of the acid-tinged saliva of a dry heave worked up into Donald's mouth. He grimaced and swallowed, took the time to dump half a package of Skittles down his throat. He maneuvered the bus back into the right direction and again ascended the hill.

At the next stop, five minutes later, Donald was still sweating and breathing heavily, not believing that someone had entrusted these kids' lives to him. Most of the remaining kids filed out, even though some of them had their stops later in the route. Donald wanted them all to leave, and he wanted to get off with them. The last in line was the boy who had jumped and cheered when Donald was hit in the head with the snowball. His face was red with anger. On his way down the stairs, the boy turned back and looked at Donald long enough for the man to see his reflection in the boy's eyes.

Donald cringed when he remembered how he had hit the accelerator while the boy was still standing. He wanted to apologize to him, maybe take him back home for hot chocolate and Nintendo games. They could be friends.

"Watch out for the ice," Donald said, hoping that the kid would laugh, as he had with his friends in back.

The boy flipped him off, and then scrambled down the stairs.

Donald jammed the gearshift into neutral. He jumped out of the bus and picked up a chunk of ice and snow, quickly smoothing out the corners. When the boy reached the end of the bus, Donald whipped the snowball. It caught the boy in the back of the neck, sending him face first into the wet ground. Donald wanted the boy to jump out of the snow and come up firing. They could split the rest of the kids on the bus into two teams and have a battle.

The boy remained on the ground for a moment, and then got up, sobbing softly. Without looking back to Donald, he picked up his books and walked home.

Donald took a deep breath, slowly climbed the stairs into the bus, and, once he was seated, rested his forehead on the steering wheel. The kids behind him whispered to one another. Donald didn't move. After a few minutes, the last of his passengers left their seats. Donald didn't look up, just sat there, one part of him exuberant over the perfect strike he had dealt the boy, another part stricken with terror over the fact that he had taken all the kids to the brink of a serious accident. He didn't move until the last child had shuffled past him, leaving him alone on the bus.

In The Hands of Heaven

The moment Steven dropped his arm onto the cold and empty spot on which Shelly was usually fast asleep at six a.m., he knew that something had changed during the night. He rolled over and checked the clock, but of course it was six; he always woke up at six.

Rubbing his eyes, he ambled towards the living room, stopping dead in the doorframe. Shelly reclined on the wide window seat, her feet hitched up, and her legs forming a triangle in front of her. She was smoking a cigarette.

Steven fell back into the shadows of the bedroom. A cigarette? He asked himself. What?

He bent forward and peered into the living room. His wife was still on the window seat, fifteen feet away, seemingly unaware that Steven was awake. He heard the slight popping sound her wet lips made as they released the butt of the cigarette. Her cheeks contracted as she took in the smoke, then fluttered outward as she exhaled, her white skin thin and fragile like a paper fan. The cigarette's fire brightened with each breath, illuminating her smooth cheeks, before wavering as she dropped her hand to her side, casting her face back into the shadow of the morning. Outside the window, fog rolled past her silhouette, its banks rising into crests and collapsing into wakes, like weary ghosts wandering invisible paths among the thick pine. The early morning sun that managed to penetrate the fog haloed her body with a dull yellow light, and, underneath her nightgown, turned her uplifted legs black.

Steven turned back to the bedroom and wiped the sweat that had formed on his forehead. A cigarette. Not his Shelly. How could it be? Their common disgust for tobacco was what had initially drawn them together. At Seward Fisheries, where they were both working, the break room was constantly filled with smoke. Only one table was designated for non-smokers, and only a few sat there. Most of the other women in the plant, Steven thought, looked more like men, with their torn jeans, flannel shirts and tattoos. They supported that image of Alaskan women Steven had while he still lived in Montana, before his uncle died and left him his property in Homer. But Shelly sat at the non-smoking table, apart from the women who told filthy jokes in the company of men and drank at the Salty Dawg Saloon after work. With such ungodly influences surrounding her, Shelly maintained her femininity, a proper amount of meekness and solemnity that was not only pleasing to Steven, but to God as well.

The night had seemed a peaceful one; Steven could not recall a bad dream, could not remember Shelly stirring in her sleep or being restless. But something had happened. His eyes darted around the dark bedroom. Nothing seemed different; no pictures were upside down, no chairs overturned. He reached for the Bible on the night-stand and flipped through the dog-eared pages. Nothing. He carefully replaced the Bible and crept to the doorway.

He watched, as her innocent breath pulled in the smoke, how the fire flared, burning even brighter and hotter in the cabin, until the flame touched his wet cheeks. His head felt light. He let it fall against the doorframe.

"Steven?" Shelly quietly asked.

He retreated into the bedroom.

"Are you awake?"

Steven stepped back into the doorframe. Shelly padded towards him and stopped a few feet away. She said nothing else, but quickly looked to the windowsill, and around the room until her gaze fell on the curio cabinet Steven had given her last Christmas. She walked to the cabinet and flicked on the light, illuminating the pieces inside, before entering the kitchen.

Steven heard the cupboards open and close, the banging of dishes and silverware. Very familiar sounds. He didn't know what to do or say. Maybe it's all my imagination, he pondered. He looked into the curio cabinet and examined the little medieval village he had been collecting for Shelly, piece by piece, since their wedding day. His favorite building, and hers, was the bakery. It was the first piece he had given her, back on the beach in Maui, a half hour after they had consummated their marriage.

The sleep was still in my eyes, Steven thought, as he went back to the bedroom to dress.

He could already taste the huckleberry pancakes and the hot coffee, the breakfast he always ate on Sunday morning. The vision of his wife smoking diminished with every step towards the kitchen. What met him at the table, however, was but a porcelain bowl, a box of corn flakes and a carton of milk.

Shelly, her back to the doorway, gazed out the window. Steven stared hard at the setting. And, when he reached for the chair he discovered that he was shaking. He gripped the chair, his knuckles hardening, and pulled it back, the legs scraping the linoleum. He sat down heavily. The wood creaked beneath his weight. He dumped the flakes in the bowl; some spilled over the lip and onto this lap. He stared absently at the milk.

"Coffee?" he blurted out.

Shelly looked over her shoulder, towards the coffee maker. She did not move immediately, not until after both had stared at it for a few moments, and Steven had begun to tap his spoon. Finally, when Steven dug into his cereal, his wife shuffled away from the window and made the coffee.

"I thought that before the prayer meeting," Steven said, "I'd chop some wood. Winter is upon us soon, God knows."

Shelly had returned to the window. Her gaze was steady. She pulled on her curled fingers as if trying to straighten them.

"What," Steven said.

Shelly looked at her hands for a moment, and then turned her eyes back to the window.

What are you looking at, Steven wanted to ask. Shelly's back was slightly bent, causing her head to droop forward. Her black hair was uncombed, and even from across the room Steven could see the circles under her eyes in the reflection of the window. She looked as if she hadn't slept in a week. Steven wanted only to feel sympathy, but now watching her nervous hands, the sight of her smoking charged into his mind.

Steven took a deep breath. He knew better than anybody the sort of temper his faith in God had helped to keep under control. He pledged to himself that nobody, especially Shelly, would ever bear his anger. If he could just wait out the day a little longer, to see what would develop. It was possible that the prayer meeting would help to resolve something. At least he and Shelly would be in the company of other good Christians who would be able to offer guidance and advice.

Steven was about to pour another serving of corn flakes when he noticed a bit of dried food on the bowl's lip. He scratched it off, only to spot a grease stain on the tablecloth.

Steven rose. Corn flakes slipped off his lap and dropped to the ground. He walked around the table, crushing the cereal under his work boots, and followed a line of grease stains on the table to the counter top next to the sink.

This is too much, he thought. Inside the sink were the dishes from the day before, the chicken grease coagulated into a sick yellow film. The plants above the sink were browning, the earth in their pots was cracked. He scanned the tiles around the flour and sugar containers and saw a dried juice puddle spotted with dead gnats. He pressed his finger against the tiles he had slaved at the fishery to buy and personally laid down on the cabinets he built. He scraped his finger towards the sink, hard enough for his skin to squeak and burn.

He lifted the finger to his eyes. It was caked with old polish and dust.

"Shelly!" he commanded.

He expected his voice to bring her to her senses, to strike fear in her heart; she was his wife.

But Shelly only raised her eyebrows and slowly turned towards her husband.

"What is this," Steven demanded, holding up his finger.

She lowered her eyebrows, but not her eyes, and kept them on Steven, unblinking and cold, as she walked past him, out of the kitchen and into the bathroom.

Steven's finger remained in the air. His face flushed, his chest heaved. He slumped into a chair, then jumped up again, walked to the living room and gently called his wife's name. She turned the water on high.

Steven backed into the dust particles tumbling through the rays of morning that were slicing through the remaining night in the room. He kept his eyes pinned to the line of yellow light burning between the bathroom door and the floor. He didn't realize his hands were trembling until he had reached the window seat, and his knuckles rapped against a pop can, knocking it to the floor. He looked down. Two cigarette butts had slipped out of the upturned can. He picked up the can and butts. He rolled the butts between his fingers. The smell of charcoal and sulfur burned his nose. He dropped the butts into the can and smashed it flat between his two big palms. He flicked the can out of his hands, as if it were too hot to hold. It bounced once off the living room rug and clattered into the hallway.

Steven dropped to his knees. He had a sudden sensation of displacement. Where am I? He wondered. The fog outside the cabin was still thick. Its movement past the window now filtered the sun's rays, laying down broken patterns of light and dark that flickered on the floor in front of Steven, as if a large fire were burning in the cold stone hearth across the room.

He looked into the hallway. The pop can rested in front of the bathroom door. He heard the sounds of his wife brushing her teeth. Her movements cast shadows on the floor, which dimpled the yellow line of light seeping beneath the bathroom door.

Steven rose and bounded through the front door. The old shack his uncle once lived in was only twenty yards from the cabin, but once Steven reached it, his cheeks were wet with sweat and tears and his legs were rubbery with fatigue. Inside were his power tools, his ax and the old furniture his uncle had left him. He hefted the ax, screamed, and buried the blade into the doorframe. The leather door hinge snapped apart like a rubber band. He could have taken apart the whole shack, smashed up the furniture and tools, knocked down the walls log by log. Instead he invoked the Lord for guidance, and once his breath began to slow, he fell into the moldy couch and sobbed like he did twenty years before when his father packed up his stuff and left Steven, his mother, and Montana for the sun and promise of Florida.

***

Two hours later, there was no more wood to split. The effort Steven threw into his chopping had soothed his spirit. He looked up at the sun and realized that the prayer meeting was only an hour away. Suddenly, Shelly popped out of the cabin. She wore a long pleated skirt and the white, cape-like jacket Steven had given her for her last birthday. Her finely brushed hair flowed over her shoulders and ended in a rounded point halfway down her back, like the fallen night sky between two snow-covered hills.

Shelly did not even look in Steven's direction, just headed down the half-mile long path that ended at the road. The ax slid out of Steven's hand. His first impulse was to run after her, but he did not even call out her name. His mind grappled with darkness, searching for something to say. He watched the shadows of the trees envelop his wife.

***

Shelly was still not home when Steven returned from the prayer meeting. He rattled through the cupboards and refrigerator, looking for something to eat. Since his wedding day, he had never had to prepare his own meal.

All through the meeting he had felt the eyes of the congregation on him and the empty chair beside him. He lied about Shelly's absence, telling everybody that she had come down with something. Nothing serious. The memory of this lie embittered his mouth. He took one bite of his peanut butter sandwich then dropped it into the sink. He drank from a carton of milk and stood in front of the window his wife had been gazing through during breakfast. Rivulets of milk ran down his chin. On Kachemak Bay, the small triangles of sailboats, like toys in a bathtub, sliced across the water. Ragged strips of cloud wrapped themselves around the Kenai peaks. Tiny storms danced across the sky-blue glaciers that were just outcroppings of enormous ice fields hidden in the heart of the mountains.

Steven saw it all, heard the birds singing in the trees and smelled the sweet wildflowers as they fell towards their graceful death before the face of autumn. The world lay before him, but from this vantage point, from the place Shelly had stood, the world was dead, without Spirit, just a reproduction of a cheap landscape painting. He searched and searched, but God was missing. He looked towards the sky and tried to see His face, but the same image kept skipping across his vision. It was Ed Harrison's face, the host of this week's prayer meeting. His lips moved slowly and emitted so sound. They didn't have to. What they said had been replaying in Steven's mind ever since he heard them.

"My wife saw her at the employment office," the voice said. "Steve, she wanted a job."

When the carton was empty, Steven let it slip to the floor. He flattened it beneath his step.

In the bedroom, he took up his Bible and headed out for the spot in the woods where he liked to read. The verses fell away from him, disappearing as soon as he read them, like freak snowflakes disintegrating on concrete warmed by the July sun. He kept returning to the same biblical passages, but his mind would not hold them. He was leaning back against a tree, the moisture of the ground long ago absorbed into his jeans.

After Ed told him about Shelly in the employment office, he had asked Steven if everything was okay at home. Steven told Ed about how good a Christian Shelly was. How she was only seventeen when they met, and how Steven knew that it was his duty to make sure Shelly remained sheltered from the evils of the world. The first thing he did, he said, was to take her away from the influences of Seward Fisheries. She was a woman. Her place was in the home. All Christians knew that. God would not have allowed the marriage if Shelly were not a good Christian, or at least capable of becoming one under Steven's guidance.

Ed had nodded and nodded. He rubbed Steven's shoulder and hugged him. Steven knew he needed somebody's help. Ed and his wife May were good Christians. Ed did what men were supposed to do on this earth, May what women were supposed to do. They were also his two closest friends. But as much as he thought he needed to, he could not bring himself to go back home and call Ed to tell him about the cigarettes and Shelly's neglect of the housework. It wasn't that he was just ashamed of Shelly's transformation; he was also frightened to admit that he, the husband, had done nothing, had just sat and watched as his wife stepped over the line. The whole morning had revealed a weakness he did not know he possessed. Ed, if he discovered it, might lead Steven to a worse revelation: that he, some-how, had fallen from God's favor.

During his stay in the woods, Shelly had been home. When Steven got back to the cabin he found a pot of spaghetti on the stove, but no note of explanation. He ate his supper directly from the pot then wandered around the cabin. He built a fire and tried to read once again from the Bible, watched part of a football game on television, simultaneously detested and fascinated by the action. He spent a half hour staring into his wife's curio cabinet. The little medieval buildings of uneven heights and irregular shapes were lined up perfectly to form an avenue that ended at the doorstep of the chapel. The last time he was in Anchorage, he had ordered his latest addition to the collection, a village inn.

Steven went to bed that night a little past his normal bedtime. He tossed and turned in his blankets for two hours. Since his wedding, he had never fallen asleep without Shelly at his side.

Finally, he heard the front door creak open. Steven knew Shelly was trying to remain quiet, but even from the bedroom he heard her soft feet tiptoe across the hardwood floor. She skipped her nightly routine in the bathroom, slipping into bed after sliding out of her clothes. Steven remained on his side, facing the other wall, opposite the door. Once she was settled, her breath regular and slow, Steven dropped his hand onto her thigh. Shelly's inhale stopped short.

"I don't want you to work," Steven said. "You know that."

Shelly remained silent for two minutes. Her thigh was hot to Ste-ven's touch. He grew hard. His hand began to inch up her thigh.

"I know," Shelly said, turning away. Steven's hand flopped to the bed.

Steven did not know that these were the last words Shelly would ever speak in his house. He lay on his back, his eyes wide open the entire night as he listened to the music of his wife's sleeping breath.

***

The Salty Dawg Saloon was beginning to thin out. It was almost midnight. Alfred, an Aleut Native and one of Steven's fellow workers from Seward Fisheries, had just slammed Charlie Connel into the plywood nailed up in front of the broken window at the front of the bar. The couple next to Steven felt each other up, a man lay passed out at their feet, and the Slime-Line Queen, a woman of questionable virtues, entangled the saloon with her high-pitched laugh. Steven's clothes stunk like smoke and his jacket was sticky with the cheap wine someone had spilled on him. He sat still for four hours though, in the hope that his wife would appear.

Steven gave up for the night. He was exhausted. He had spent the morning mangling pink salmon at Seward Fisheries. He had a tough enough time gutting the small, mushy fish on a good day. Today, his large hands trembling, he ripped through the fragile spines of most of the fish that came his way. He clocked himself out at noon and went home. Shelly wasn't there. Nor was she at the employment office, or Ed's house. Thinking the worse, he had ended up at the Salty Dawg.

When Steven opened the front door of the bar, he was met with a blast of wind rolling off Kachemak Bay. The impact brought tears to his eyes. He continued walking, wiping them away. Someone bumped into him.

"Jesus, sorry, Jack," the man said.

Steven looked up. The man hesitated before moving on. His eyes shifted. Did Steven know him?

"Excuse me," Steven said, brushing past him. He didn't think much of the interchange until he was pulled out of his thoughts by the sputtering of a pick-up that had just been parked; the engine, in dire need of a tune-up, popped and snapped. Steven stopped. The truck's bed was full and covered with a tarp. Steven looked back. The front door of the Salty Dawg swung open. The couple that had been sitting next to Steven inside stepped out, arm in arm. The man quickly pinned the woman to the side of the building, dropped to his knees and began tugging on her belt with his teeth; she laughed and gently slapped his head away.

Steven turned away in disgust.

***

Steven tripped over the box sitting right inside the door of his cabin, jarring him out of the stupor he'd been in since leaving the Salty Dawg. The box itself he paid no heed. The cold and dark cabin had changed somehow. He couldn't place the feeling, whether it was the quick rush of familiarity one's hit with upon returning home after a long vacation, or the feeling that an alien presence had invaded, an intruder, not necessarily taking or touching anything, but leaving behind an indelible presence.

Steven jumped over the box and ran into the bedroom. He swung open Shelly's closet and groped inside. Nothing.

Heartbeat and breath quickening with each step, he fumbled his way into the bathroom and tore the drawers away from the vanity. Their contents spilled to the floor. He tossed the drawers aside and fell to his knees. He tried to pick up the various bottles and tubes, but his hands couldn't manage it. He scattered containers and toilet articles all over the floor. Nothing of Shelly's remained.

Steven lurched back into the main room. The box sat in a square of moonlight. He charged up to it and tore wildly at the brown paper. He took the village inn in his trembling fingers, allowing the box to fall and the Styrofoam packing to float to the ground.

"It's hers," he said. "She brought it in, but didn't open the box."

Steven spun around and threw the inn across the room and into the curio cabinet. The rounded glass door shattered in a curtain of shards. The inn plowed into the rest of the village, spinning away from the chapel. Some of the buildings slid off the shelf and exploded into ceramic chunks and dust on the floor. The chapel remained in its place.

The destruction calmed Steven for a brief moment. He leaned back against the door pane. His mind became clear enough for him to scan back through his memories for some clue.

The sputtering truck at the Salty Dawg. The loaded bed. The man who bumped into him and his strange look. Steven swayed and clutched his pounding head. He fell back through the front door, into the night, and went for the ax.

***

Dispersed moonlight broke through the trees in a shower of diamonds. Steven had been down this path a thousand times before, but now, at a clumsy run, his body intoxicated with rage, his mind couldn't place the exposed roots, the low boughs. The branches tore at his clothes, the slippery ground at his ankles. The ax, however, was firmly in hand.

He descended towards the road. He would go to the Salty Dawg. For his wife. He ran, staggered. He fell to his knees, crawled a few feet, something biting into his hand. He was up again and a branch took him across the eye. But he brushed aside the pain. He was gaining momentum, could make out the road through the trees. His heartbeat clanged in his rib cage like a bell. He held the ax so tightly he could no longer feel his grip. A sharp pain tore into his leg, right above the ankle. He twisted, fell, not to his knees, but to his side and off the path, down what seemed like an endless slope. He rolled like a stripped log, taking with him small plants, wildflowers, overripe berries, twigs, rocks, bear scat, mud. Something bit into his arms, straight through his jacket. But it wasn't painful. Nothing was. There was just the long fall. Then he hit bottom, his back to the cold ground. The moon was full and the light felt like salt in his eyes. He jerked away from the light and buried his face into his hands.

He was in his neighbor's yard, a junkyard, a myriad of rusting appliances. A barking dog moved Steven back to his feet. In moments he was on the road for the Salty Dawg. He still had the ax. His arm was sliced open and the drying blood plastered sleeve to skin. His clothes were covered with undergrowth and bear scat. He limped. He didn't try to hitch-hike. The miles back to the Salty Dawg were nothing. Still, after only minutes on the road, a pick-up stopped beside him. Without hesitation, Steven jumped into the bed. The truck idled for a moment before speeding on. There was only the one road, the last road, the one that ended at the tip of Homer Spit in the middle of Kachemak Bay. At such a late hour, there was only the Salty Dawg.

"You need a drink, buddy," a voice said. It was the driver. The truck was in front of the Salty Dawg. Five miles, just like that.

"A drink," Steven said. He crawled over the tailgate and fell to his unsteady feet.

"God bless you," he told the driver.

"Sure, what the hell." The truck ripped into the parking lot, spitting out gravel and clamshells from beneath its wheels.

Pick-ups were everywhere. But the one Steven remembered hadn't moved. The loaded bed. The tarp. He went to the truck and with his ax cut the ropes holding down the tarp. He cut all the connections. He pulled the tarp off and stared. He stared at his wife's possessions for more minutes than he could account for. A chorus of voices and footsteps approached.

"Her clothes are in this box," Steven said. "And here's the rocking chair her grandmother refinished. That's her bureau."

The steps got closer.

"This box has kitchen appliances. And I can see the heads of her stuffed animals sticking out of that box."

A rough, callused hand grabbed Steven's wrist. Without a flinch, Steven reversed the grip and shoved a man he didn't recognize to the ground.

"Those are the candlesticks we bought in Fairbanks."

"Steven?"

It was Shelly.

"Steven, why don't you put the ax down?"

"Shelly, these are your things. Why are your things in this truck? This isn't our truck. We don't have a truck."

Shelly stepped forward. She wore a pink waitress's uniform.

"Jesus, not too close, Shell," a man said. "Look at him. Whattya been doin', Jack? Wrestling an outhouse?"

"These things should be in our cabin, Shelly."

"I'm sorry, Steven."

"Sorry?" Steven had to be nearer to Shelly. He stepped closer.

The man who had bumped into Steven earlier stood next to Shelly.

"Take it easy there, fella," he said. "We don't need trouble. I'm just a friend, helping out."

"Shelly, I..." The ax Steven held behind his back began to shake. Sweat popped out of his forehead. He didn't take his eyes from Shelly. She stood firm and silent. From the side of Steven's vision, a small cloud of smoke appeared and rolled into Shelly's face.

"Jesus, sorry, Shell. It's a helluva habit."

Shelly didn't fan the smoke away. A tear glistened in the corner of her eye and rolled down her cheek.

Steven let out a choked cry. He dropped the ax and fell to the ground, into a crumpled mass, at Shelly's feet.

"Oh, Shelly..." Steven started. "Oh, God. God forgive me."

Shelly turned, without another word, and climbed into the pick-up truck.

Substitutions

Donald was nineteen, male, and a virgin. The choice should be obvious. Turn left and fall into the arms of a beautiful, unhappily married woman, or turn right and play video games, yet again, with a bitter old man who not only claims responsibility for the death of your dad, but bawls you out for everything you do. Those friends of his who were preparing to complete their first year at the university in Anchorage would call him a fag for even hesitating. But like every other night he came to this crossroads, Donald turned right.

Hopkins was already drunk. The old man had a shotgun, instead of his hunting rifle, trained on Donald. At such a close range, even with a wavering barrel, Hopkins would be able to hit him with at least a couple buckshot pellets.

"It's just me, old man," Donald said. "Put the gun down."

"I ain't got time for nobody," Hopkins said. "Who is it?"

Hopkins' house was a rusted out mobile home with a plywood addition nailed up in front of the only door. Thick black smoke poured from a wrought iron chimney that had been welded to the trailer's roof. Most of the windows were boarded up. Hopkins was standing in the doorway of the addition; his old dog, with sad brown eyes, peeked out between her master's legs. The space between the road and the house was littered with empty oil barrels, rotted box traps, stiff gray fishing nets pressed into the mud and snow, broken bicycles, splintered two-by-fours, a couple of salt licks, a washing machine with its front panel torn off, as well as an assortment of garden tools green with age and disuse. It looked as if Hopkins had buried a whole junk yard over the course of the winter, and now as spring approached, the warming sun forced the items out of the shrinking snow pack like tulip bulbs in a pot of white moss. Donald didn't know why Hopkins kept all this crap.

"Put the gun down, old man," Donald said. "And let's get drunk." He held a bottle of rum in the air.

"I ain't got time for nobody," Hopkins said. "I coulda blasted you apart." He dropped the barrel of the gun and went back inside. The dog stayed in the doorway and wagged her tail as Donald approached. Part of her ear was missing, and as she led Donald into the trailer, he noticed that the poor thing had a new limp; she was always getting attacked by cats, chased down by grizzlies, and trampled by moose.

"Hey, Suzy Q," Donald said, patting her head.

The trailer, as usual, was dim, but little LED lights pinpricked the gloom with small points of reds, yellows and greens; the place was crammed with Nintendo games, telephones, answering machines, a sprawling stereo system, televisions, remote control airplanes, boats and cars, an artificial Christmas tree, a microwave, blenders, ice cream and milk shake machines, just about anything Hopkins could order from the JC Penney catalog.

"Spiced rum," Hopkins said. "What kind of kiddie-girlie drink is that? Why don't you get the hell out and come back with a bottle of whiskey?"

Donald didn't answer, just went to the kitchen for two glasses. He always brought Captain Morgan's; Hopkins always drank it.

Donald started coming here six months earlier, in September. He had spent the summer on a transcontinental trip with a buddy, driving to Florida, and then back to Alaska. They were working their way home, camped deep in the outback of Jasper National Park in Alberta, when Donald's father was pitched off the side of his fishing boat by a fierce gust of wind.

After the accident, the people of Homer flocked to Donald, offering him sympathy and all kinds of advice. Most thought he should stay in town and continue fishing Cook Inlet on his father's boat. Some suggested he sell the boat and house, go off to college and start a new life. The owner of "Video Round-up," a divorced woman of forty-three, offered adoption, without all the papers, on account of Donald being a legal adult. Before the accident, Donald had planned on going to college in Anchorage, and in the summers, helping his father out on the boat. A straight path through life was clear in front of him. But with the news of his father's death, his view into the future went black.

He became paralyzed. When the school year started, his buddies went off to college. Donald stayed in Homer and took a job as a school bus driver, planning to work at Seward Fisheries in the summer. In the middle of September, Hopkins called.

"I bet you need to get drunk," he had said. "Only thing to do is try to forget it for a while."

Hopkins' reputation of bitterness preceded him. Among the children of Homer, he was seen as a type of witch, wander too close to his house and he'd shoot you, then lock you into a dark closet, a type of pickling stage before feeding you to his dog. But of all the advice Donald had been given, Hopkins' was the soundest; the old man was a loner, and Donald held more loneliness than grief. Drinking with someone who felt the same way seemed like a good way to handle it.

That first visit, as winter began to tease Homer with increasingly consistent frosts and flurries, Donald went out to Hopkins' place, along the way remembering how his father used to give him a beer or two after a hard day's fishing, the laughs they had together, only to be met with the barrel of Hopkins' gun.

"Get out before I blast ya!" Hopkins shouted.

Donald ran home. Hopkins called a half hour later.

"Where the hell are you?" he asked

"You had your gun out," Donald said. "You were going to shoot me."

"Don't be stupid," Hopkins said. "How the hell was I supposed to know it was you? I ain't seen you since you was a kid."

So Donald went back, only to find Hopkins mad because he hadn't brought something to drink.

"Damn charity case," Hopkins mumbled, reaching behind a television for a half-empty bottle of Jack Daniel's.

Donald, occasionally looking towards the closet and Suzy-Q, was scared the whole time he was there. He took tentative sips of his whiskey, letting Hopkins do most of the drinking and talking.

"Your daddy couldn't fish out of a loaded bucket," Hopkins said. "It's no wonder he fell off the damn boat."

Donald turned red in the face, his eyes growing shiny with tears.

Hopkins shifted his legs around the couch, let his yellowing eyes search the peeling walls of his trailer.

"Nothing wrong with the boat when I sold it to him," he said, now studying his glass. "Still isn't." He looked towards Donald, his wet lips parted, eyes like his dog's.

For sixth months they had been drinking together, sometimes four or five times a week. Now Donald brought his own liquor, brushed off Hopkins' paranoia, and played with Suzi-Q more than the old man did. He returned from the kitchen with two glasses and the bottle of Captain Morgan's.

"Hell, I thought you were that fruitcake Born Again," Hopkins said. "Almost blasted ya."

Donald sat down in an easy chair. In front of him was a pile of old dog shit that was collapsing into white dust.

"I just don't believe that guy could be a relative of John's," Hopkins said, taking up his drink.

John had been Hopkins' neighbor and best friend for over thirty years. The Born Again inherited the land after John's death.

"He's always knocking on my door, trying to convert me," Hopkins said. "No, I don't think he could be a relative. Maybe I should go up there and run him off that property. He'd be trespassing."

Hopkins stood, looking around for the gun he had set down moments before.

"Sit down and drink your drink, old man," Donald said. He first met Shelly, the Born Again's beautiful, unhappy wife, after Hopkins took a shot at her. The two men were watching a movie when Hopkins heard a twig snap outside. He went out with his shotgun and fired into the woods. Donald was shocked. He jumped out of his chair and ran outside. Hopkins was standing with his gun lowered, wiping his wet eyes because he had just blown apart a newly planted sapling.

"What did you shoot!" Donald shouted.

"On my property," Hopkins muttered.

Donald peered into the woods. A fluttering, yellow figure, like a bed sheet hung out to dry in the wind, floated between the trees. He sprinted around the junk in the yard and caught up with Shelly. The moon cut through the branches, shining on her like a spotlight so that her face was snow white, her lips red as broken cranberries. She wore a nightgown, the triangle of her cleavage a shadow falling beneath the bright yellow fabric.

"Are you okay?" Donald asked in a trembling voice. Her black hair, glistening in the moonlight, lay like feathers on her shoulders. He was in awe of her.

"He could have killed you," Donald said, wiping the sweat from his lips. "Aren't you scared?"

Her face was blank. She continued walking, stepping carefully around exposed roots.

"My name is Donald," he said. "What's yours?"

She turned around.

"I'm married."

"You live up there?" he asked, pointing toward the cabin the Born Again had built.

"Why do you ask?" she said.

"Just wondering," Donald said. "I'm over at Hopkins' all the time. We'll probably see more of each other."

"You're drunk," she said.

Donald rubbed his neck and blushed. He was too embarrassed to say anything else and had to turn around to hide the erection that pressed at his jeans. He began walking back to the mobile home. When he reached the edge of Hopkins' yard, she called after him.

"We probably will," she said.

Donald turned around, but she was already well up the slope towards her cabin.

The very next morning, at four a.m., she called him at the one room cabin he'd been living in since his father's death.

"I want to see you," she said, in a trembling voice that seemed to be of naked, experienced lust, years beyond the murmurings and pleadings Donald had shared in the back of cars, on the deck of his father's boat, on the couch in darkened living rooms with the blushing, tentative girls he knew from high school.

That was months ago. At this moment, as Hopkins once again berated the Born Again, Donald didn't realize that the voice on the phone hadn't been brimming with lust, but with imploring desperation. He hadn't yet found the courage to take the left path up to the Born Again's cabin, even though he presumed that Shelly's offer was still open.

Hopkins gave up looking for his gun and fell back into the sofa to finish his drink.

"Homer's going to hell," he said. "First it was those long hairs, coming up here with their tie-dyes and health food. Trying to keep McDonald's out of here. Hell, I love a Big Mac. Now it's these Jesus freaks, shoving their Bible in my face. They're behind the Spill, I say, shitting up our water."

"That guy up there," Hopkins said, lazily waving his right hand. "He takes the cake. I don't think shooting him will learn him a lesson. I think I'll have to take the barrel to his head, scramble up his brains some."

Hopkins drank his rum, and then poured another.

"Say, my boy," he said in an even tone. "Why don't you hump his wife already?"

"Jesus," Donald said, turning his head toward the kitchen.

"Seriously," Hopkins said. "I think it would do her some good. She's meek as hell. You know that guy knocks her around. She's just looking for a way off that place."

"I don't know what you're talking about."

"Shit, I don't. Take a few years off of me, and I'd be on her like a wolf on a wounded fawn."

Donald stood with his drink and cigarette, and walked over to an un-boarded window. Suzy-Q followed him and licked something off his pant leg.

"You know what your problem is," Hopkins said.

"What," Donald said, not turning around.

"Hell, it's not too hard to figure out," Hopkins said. "You're always here getting drunk instead of getting some. I remember my first one. A whore in Germany. I think she must have had this disease up her nose, because every time she breathed it sounded like someone rubbing two pine cones together. Be different for you. Shelly'll be sweet as Juji-fruits."

Donald swung around, splashing Suzy-Q with rum.

"You're a pig," he said, grabbing the bottle. He poured his glass full and turned back to the window. Hopkins was silent for as long as it took Donald to finish his drink. Then the Nintendo machine turned on with a "ping!" A crowd roared. It was the football game. Donald's favorite.

"I beat your high score in 'Galaga' the other day," Hopkins said.

Donald reached down and petted the dog.

"I don't believe that," he said. He walked back to Hopkins and sat down in front of the television. The old man poured him another drink and handed him the other joystick.

"Beat your ass in football, too," Hopkins said.

They played video games well into the afternoon, and later on watched a hockey game. The fifth of rum was gradually consumed.

Donald waited all day for Hopkins to bring up the boat; the old man always managed to. During the evening news the weatherman predicted a quick end to the warm spell; the Kenai Peninsula would be back in the grasp of winter within hours.

"Storm's coming," Hopkins said. "Their damn radar pictures don't do it justice. I should go down and check on your boat, make sure it's lashed down steady."

Hopkins knew as well as Donald that nothing less than a tsunami could rock waves into Homer Harbor.

"Don't worry about it," Donald said.

"The hell I won't worry about it. I've been taking care of that boat ever since your daddy died. Painted it, rebuilt the engine. You should see it some time."

"Next time I see it," Donald said, "I'll sell it."

"Now what do you want to go and do that for?" Hopkins said. "Why, me and John practically built that boat from scratch. Sold it to your Daddy for practically nothing, too."

"The boat hasn't been used since...you know," Donald said.

"It still runs fine."

"I could use the money for college."

"You ain't going away to no college."

Donald had no reply for that. He refilled the glasses and settled down in front of the television. Reruns flew by his eyes like a merry-go-round. Before he knew it, the clock struck nine and the bottle was just about empty. Neither he nor Hopkins had said a word since the news.

"It was my fault," Donald drawled. "Not yours."

"Eh?"

"My fault. If I hadn't gone on that damn trip, it would have been me. I thought the Spill threw everyone out of work. I thought there'd be plenty of workers. But they all left to be on the clean-up crews. More money."

"I built the damn boat," Hopkins said.

"I could have gone and helped with the net instead of Dad doing it."

"I built the whole thing," Hopkins said. Tears were starting to roll down his cheeks. He blew his nose on his sleeve. "Something went wrong with that damn pulley and it wasn't the first time. I shoulda caught it before he went out."

He emptied the bottle into his glass.

"It's my fault Dad died," Donald said.

Hopkins drank his rum in one gulp. He dropped the glass on the table and began to waver. His eyes rolled back in his head, and he fell back onto the couch.

"Hopkins," Donald whispered.

The old man didn't respond. Donald kicked him in the knee.

"Go get another bottle," Donald said.

Hopkins didn't budge. Donald watched the old man's chest for movement, just as Donald's father said he used to do when he was a baby in the crib.

It seemed like an eternity since the old man's last breath.

"Hopkins!" Donald seized the old man by his shoulders.

"Hopkins! Wake up!" Donald shook him as if he were a disobedient child. He was about to slap him when Hopkins sputtered and a bit of drool slid down his chin.

"What the hell ya doing," Hopkins said. "Get off me. I ain't your lovebird. I ain't your daddy."

Donald let go. He discovered that he had been crying.

"I need a drink," Hopkins said.

Donald backed away. He and Hopkins had downed the whole bottle of rum, but he didn't feel drunk. Just a dull ache lurked in his head behind his ears. He wiped away the tears with his shirtsleeve.

"Sometimes I wish I was your daddy," Hopkins said.

"What for?" Donald asked, still sniffling.

"So I's could tell you what a fuck up you are."

"You tell me that anyway."

"Not enough. Look at you. All you do is get drunk and drive a school bus around. You think your daddy would put up with that? He'd smack you one, is what he'd do."

"Nuh-uh," Donald bleated out. He wanted to get up and leave, but instead cowered in the easy chair. He felt small, like he had when his father was about to bust his ass for smoking, or for running over a flowerbed with the lawn mower.

"Like hell he wouldn't," Hopkins said. "You think he taught you to fish for nothing? All you do is flounder around, wait for the world to come to you. You're a man now. Act like one! Go out there and fuck anything that moves. And when you're not fucking, make yourself rich."

The heat was starting to rise up Donald's back. He nudged the table with his foot and eyed the whiskey bottle.

"You're the one to talk," he said.

"Get serious, boy," Hopkins said. "I'm seventy, for Chrissake. The Good Lord could take me now I won't cry about it.

"You," he finished, "are only nineteen."

Donald shot out of the chair and paced around the room, pulling hard on his cigarette; the tobacco sparked and crackled, and ashes were swept onto his cheeks.

"What are you trying to do to me?" he asked, his voice breaking.

"Nothing," Hopkins said. "I'm just talking."

Donald stamped out his cigarette on an aluminum windowsill and slumped back into the easy chair. Suzy-Q followed and placed her chin on his knee.

"I need another drink," Donald said.

"Nobody's forcing you," Hopkins said.

They gazed at their empty glasses.

Finally, Hopkins stood.

"You can do whatever the hell you want," he said.

"Where are you going?" Donald asked.

"I'm going down to the harbor to check on the boat. Come along if you want."

"Why don't you just leave the boat alone," Donald said. "Just leave it."

"Can't let the fuel lines freeze," Hopkins said. "You just can't leave a thing like a boat slumping around. You got to take care of it."

"That's not what I mean," Donald said. "Besides, even I know you don't keep liquid fuel in this time of year."

Hopkins stopped at the door, coat in hand.

"That's not what I mean," Donald repeated softly.

He put his face in his hands, covering his eyes. Everything turned black. From nowhere came streaking bullets of light that bounced off his eyes, then disappeared, leaving a view of Kachemak Bay in its wake. Donald is standing on Homer Spit Beach while the fishing boat returns, its hold so heavy with Red salmon the hull is sunk treacherously low in the water, and his father, arms crossed, legs apart, seems not to be standing on the deck, but on the choppy waves. As the boat rounds the tip of the spit to enter the harbor, its running lights glowing dimly against the wooded foothills of the Kenai Range, it suddenly spirals out of control. Donald is no longer on the beach, but on the boat, behind the wheel, when his father goes overboard.

The image still plastered in front of his mind's eye, Donald burst into tears. He cried like he never cried before, not when his mother left Alaska, or when he first heard of his father's death.

Hopkins shuffled back to the couch and sat down. He looked around at all his gadgets and machines, then fumbled for the bottle and shook a few remaining drops into Donald's glass.

"Jesus, Hopkins," Donald said. "He came out black. He passed through that damn spill and washed up on the beach stained black. Jesus Christ."

"I know, son. I know, damn it all."

Donald looked at his glass. He tried to remember the last time he had held someone, or someone had held him. Was it at his father's funeral? Someone must have hugged him, but he couldn't remember whom. He had the sudden urge to hug Hopkins, even though he had never done it before. Donald reached out to touch him.

"I'll get another bottle," Hopkins said, standing up and moving towards the kitchen.

"I've had enough," Donald said, trying to hide the disappointment in his voice.

Hopkins stopped.

"I really didn't mean to stay so long," Donald said. "I thought I'd take up that offer from the Born Again's wife, give her a call."

Hopkins sighed deeply, and then put his hand on the wall.

"You can't do that," he said.

That was the last response Donald expected.

"Why not?"

"Just think about it," Hopkins said. "How's she going to explain it to that nut-job of a husband?"

"Yeah, you're right, maybe tomorrow..."

"Course, I am. I'll call."

"What?"

Hopkins leapt back to the couch, whistling along the way. The booze he'd been putting back, as well as his fit, seemed to be history. He reached down and shuffled through a stack of crumpled up pieces of paper.

"Now, don't you worry. Ol' Hopkins will take care of you. Just shut up a minute."

Hopkins squinted at a soiled piece of paper and punched out a number on one of his telephones.

"Hey, you," he said into the receiver. "Born Again! It's me, Hopkins...No, this ain't no prank...Why don't you bring your Bible down here so we's can have a talk...What do you mean, what for? So's you can talk to me about getting saved. The Good Lord's calling for me, I tell ya...Yes, I'm serious, Goddamn it. Don't I sound it? Okay."

Hopkins hung up.

"Now, hurry up," he said. "He'll be here any minute."

Mark Lewandowski

"Are you sure about this?" Donald asked.

"What, you too?" Hopkins said. "The fruitcake'll come down the main path. You'll have to skirt around the back so he don't see you. Jesus, hurry. I don't know how long I'll be able to listen to his jabber before I smack him one."

"I appreciate it," Donald said, putting on his cap. "I appreciate all you've done for me."

"Your daddy was a good man," Hopkins said. "Wait a sec." He trotted to the back of the trailer and rummaged through a dresser next to the bed, then met Donald at the door.

"Here," he said, handing Donald a condom. The package was nearly disintegrated.

Hopkins rubbed his chin and looked above Donald's shoulder, as if searching for something to say. He reached out his hand slowly, giving Donald's arm three quick pats.

"You know what to do with it?" Hopkins asked.

"I think so."

"Good boy. Now, git!"

As Hopkins instructed, Donald approached the cabin from the back, up a steep slope. The stone chimney on the roof coughed thick, black smoke. All the blinds were drawn open. Yellow flashes of light poured out of the windows, sending dancing shadows into the dark forest. Donald crept up to the nearest window and looked in. The light was coming from a furious fire in a large stone hearth in the middle of the main room. Shelly was perched on a large window seat across the room, her back against the side wall and her legs stretched out in front of her. Her head drooped to one side. Her right arm hung down. Her hand and the tips of her fingers were wavering, as if in reaction to a small breeze. She wore the same yellow nightgown she had the night he first met her, but now, the curve of her breasts and the motion of her chest were lost in the folds of the cloth and her slumping neck. She looked like a doll that would only go into motion with the turn of a key.

She's a goddess, Donald thought. He crept to the front door and knocked gently. When he heard nothing beyond the door, he knocked with greater urgency. The door swung open and there she stood. The cold air made her nipples erect immediately.

"Yes?" she asked.

"It's me, Donald. Don't you remember?" She looked much younger know, in the full light. Donald thought that she probably wasn't much older than he.

"Of course. I just saw you, right after your friend shot at me."

"Well, yeah, that was six months ago."

"Was it?"

"Yeah, remember? You called me later that night?"

"Of course."

"Your husband's talking to Hopkins."

"Is he? You better come in then."

Donald slipped out of his boots and left them on the stoop.

"I'm married," Shelly said.

"Yeah," Donald said, following her into the cabin, which was uncomfortably warm. "Nice place."

"My husband built it all by himself."

"He probably wouldn't want me here."

"No, he wouldn't."

This is stupid, Donald thought. What was I thinking? This woman's as nutty as her husband.

"Maybe I'll see you around," Donald said, turning back to the door.

"Aren't we going to make love first?" Shelly asked. "That is what you came here for, isn't it?"

"Yeah," Donald said, turning back to face her. Her nightgown lay crumpled at her feet. Now she wore only a pair of white panties. Her skin was white, practically translucent. Donald had spent many nights imagining this moment. He had been afraid of staring at her breasts, once he saw them out like this. But he took only a quick look. He couldn't look for long at any part of her, just averted his eyes to a point above her right shoulder.

"Shouldn't we have a drink or something?" he asked.

"My husband doesn't drink, you silly. We can smoke afterwards. Just don't tell my husband. He doesn't know I smoke."

"Okay," Donald said, unsure of what to do. Shelly stepped toward him. Donald retreated, but after a step he was against the wall.

"Don't be afraid," Shelly said.

"I've never done it, with a married woman, I mean."

"Oh? It works the same way," Shelly said. "We take off all our clothes, kiss, then you lay on top of me."

She was inches from him. She took his shaking hands and placed them on her breasts. He closed his eyes and tried to concentrate on the softness of her skin and the points of his palms where the tips of her nipples pressed into him. He should have an erection then. But he couldn't lose himself in the moment. He couldn't stop thinking about the first time he pinned his father in a wrestling match in the backyard. The memory popped in his head and wouldn't go away. When his father was bent over, weeding the watermelon patch, Donald snuck up behind and got him in a headlock. His father tried to twist out of his grasp, but he couldn't stop laughing. His head was pressed into Donald's face and the smell of shampoo overpowered him. This is what Donald now smelled. Not the pine crackling in the fireplace, or the mustiness emanating from Shelly.

"Do you want to touch me down there now?" Shelly asked.

Donald opened his eyes. His hands were still on her breasts.

"What? No, I mean, yes, but in a few minutes," Donald said. "I forgot my condoms." He reached for the doorknob.

"Did you?"

"I'll be right back, I promise. Have a smoke."

"Can I?" Shelly asked. She stepped back into the main room of the cabin and slipped into her nightgown.

Donald slammed the door behind him and jumped into his boots, not bothering to lace them up. Before sliding down the slope to Hopkins' property, he peeped into the window once again. Shelly had resumed her position on the window seat across the room. The only difference now was that one hand held a cigarette. She looked lonelier than he had ever felt. He knew he couldn't alleviate her loneliness by having sex with her, anymore than she could help him make sense of his life. Ever since he first masturbated at the age of twelve he had spent half his waking moments thinking of an encounter with such a beautiful woman. She threw himself at him. He could have lost his virginity. Finally. But he ran, and he would never go back. He was relieved to find out that it didn't matter to him, that there were things more important.

At the bottom of the slope, Donald smashed through the crusted snow. An excited voice, sounding thin in the cold, still air, came from the addition's door.

Born Again, Donald thought. He sat down on a tree stump. Still affected by the bright yellow fire in Shelly's cabin, his eyes were just now growing accustomed to the failing light. Black mangled shapes, rising out of the white ground, appeared in front of him. He knew they were only rusting stoves and refrigerators, but he imagined them being rocks on a beach stained black with oil, and somewhere in this forest of junk, his father's body lay. Three days it took the bloated body to wash up on the beach south of Anchor Point, but not before passing through the slick seeping in from Prince William Sound.

Donald would have remained where he was all night if the Born Again's voice hadn't been replaced by Hopkins' wild, cackling laugh.

"I miss you," Donald said.

The laughing continued. Donald sat back on the stump and grinned, but when he realized that the Born Again was probably losing ground with Hopkins, and that he'd be coming out of the door any moment, he jumped up from the stump and darted toward the road.

***

Donald had thought the sight of the boat would fill him with terror. Instead, he felt a great sense of relief. Hopkins must have worked on it earlier, and had planned on coming back later because the tarp was folded and placed in the lifeboat. The entire shell of the boat had been repainted, the deck stripped and weatherproofed, and the pulley system that had snagged and forced his father from behind the wheel replaced.

Donald hopped down into the boat; it rocked gently beneath his feet. Keeping his hand on the railing, he walked with careful steps towards the cabin. He placed his hands on the ladder next to the door, its fine grain smooth to the touch, and leapt up to the wheelhouse.

It wasn't at all like he remembered it. The brass fixtures and steel controls were polished and sparkling. The glass protecting the gauges was clear. The wheel had been sanded down and re-stained. There was no grease, no beer cans, no fruit cores, no candy wrappers.

He approached the wheel. The antique had been his father's own addition. Donald gazed at it, remembered the first time he was allowed to steer, his father behind him, goading him with quiet, confident words, and how, eventually, his father left him alone in the wheel house, and let him captain the boat. Soon, they were like partners, sharing the blame when the take was thin, celebrating together when the hold was full, every summer the wheel working to shrink the gap between adult and child, until, six months ago, when the wheel tore them apart.

Donald expected the wheel to be heavy and warm with grief, but the wood felt cool and familiar. Hopkins was right, of course; his father taught him to be a fisherman. He knew nothing else, nor did he want anything else. The wheel, with its past of pain and love, contained his future as well.

He reached into his pocket for the key he had never taken off the chain. He leaned forward and started the boat. The engine's hum was smooth and soft. He smiled, thinking of Hopkins, and put his hand back on the wheel. He spun it gently, a few degrees in one direction, a few in the other. The wheel was perfectly balanced.

About the Author

Mark Lewandowski writes stories, essays, and screenplays. In addition to sliming fish in Alaska, he has served as a Peace Corps Volunteer in Poland, and taught American Studies and Creative Writing as a Fulbright Scholar in Lithuania. He completed his MFA in Creative Writing at Wichita State University. Currently, he lives in Terre Haute, where he teaches at Indiana State University.

FOR MORE INFORMATION ON TITLES AVAILABLE FROM
ALL THINGS THAT MATTER PRESS, GO TO
http://allthingsthatmatterpress.com
or contact us at
allthingsthatmatterpress@gmail.com

www.ingramcontent.com/pod-product-compliance
Lightning Source LLC
Chambersburg PA
CBHW032138270626
47172CB00008B/355

9 780984 421930